Heidi Garrett

the Tree Hugger

A Dystopian Fairy Tale

The Tree Hugger by Heidi Garrett
Half-Faerie Publishing

Copyright © 2014 by Heidi Garrett

Find out more about Heidi Garrett at
www.heidigwrites.blogspot.com

Cover Art by J.W.B.

Editing by Vince Dickinson

ISBN: 978-0-9882068-7-8

Other Books by Heidi Garrett

Sign up for Heidi's newsletter!
http://eepurl.com/wWKUj

Daughter of Light

(A Young Adult Fantasy Trilogy)

Isolt's Enchantment, A Prequel
Half Faerie, #1
Half Mortal, #2
War & Grace, #3

Once Upon a Time Today

(A Collection of Stand-Alone Modern Fairy Tale Retellings)

The Girl Who Believed in Fairy Tales: Three Short Stories
Beautiful Beautiful
Dreaming of the Sea
I Am Lily Dane

In Collaboration with Billie Limpin

(A New Adult Paranormal Romance)

Cupcakes and Kisses

To the trees who steadfastly provide us

fresh air.

Contents

long time ago ❁ 1

one ❁ 3

two ❁ 21

three ❁ 33

four ❁ 57

five ❁ 81

six ❁ 105

seven ❁ 121

eight ❁ 145

nine ❁ 163

ten ❁ 177

Author's Note ❁ 181

Thank You ❁ 183

First Chapter of I Am Lily Dane ❁ 185

About the Author ❁ 195

long time ago

Long time ago, a man wrote a story about women who lived in trees—or with trees—maybe on account of trees. Little Mother gave me a copy of the story on one of my birthdays, same as Ma gave her. It dug deep into my mind then sank farther down, into my soul. Then, it was like the story became a part of my skin and bones. It got to where whenever the wind picked up my hair and tossed it around, I'd imagine my head covered with leaves and my toes rooted in the good earth. All this made me think harder about Ma and her forest farm, and Little Mother and her zeal to preach.

This is the passage that really speaks to me:

The Dryad felt herself irresistibly drawn into the dance. Her small, delicate feet were shod in silken shoes as brown as the ribbon that fluttered from her hair onto her bare shoulders. The large folds of the green silk dress enveloped her, but could not hide the perfectly shaped legs and dainty feet, which seemed to be trying to draw a magic circle in the air before her dancing cavalier's head. Was she in the enchanted garden of Armida? What was the name of this place? In bright gas flames outside shown the name Mabille.

There were shouts and applause, rockets and running water, and the popping of champagne bottles. The dance was Bacchanalian, wild.—Hans Christian Andersen

The story doesn't say the dryad mated with the cavalier, but from my understanding, those kinda details weren't talked about back then.

I keep asking myself, what if she did?

—Magnolia Lee Winthrop, 2160

one

Mags

The fire's flames leap into the night sky like hope.

I'm settled on a log, with Ma on one side of me and Graham on the other. Me and Graham are seven years old. Graham's Pa is on the other side of him. Graham and his Pa are sad inside cause Graham's ma died. Being sad inside is something I know about, so I never repeat things like: She's in a better place, or Just be happy you had the time with her that you did. Sometimes it's better to just sit quiet with a person. Sometimes that's all they need to keep the black hole of grief madness at a distance.

"There wouldn't be a single dictator in the world, cause everyone on the planet would have the right to defend themselves and the ones they love. Every community would grow their own vegetable gardens and have enough acres for grazing livestock. We don't need much meat, just enough to fit in the center of our palm each day." Ma holds out her hand in the firelight.

I gaze at her long, slim fingers that look so much like mine. I lean against her, and that hand comes around my back and squeezes my shoulder. I shut my eyes so I can take in the comfort of her touch. I let her voice seep in, too.

"And there would be plenty of butter to kill the cancer cells that are always mutating inside of us. Pfff. Margarine cain't do that. Plus, with everyone eating enough fat, their brains would work right. Who knows what the human race would be capable of if every person's brain worked at optimum? We could probly harness energy that wouldn't pollute the air we breathe or water we drink."

Ma's words become a lullaby, and before I know it, she's shaking me awake.

The night is cold now that the fire's out.

Ma's got a jar in her hand. It's filled with fruit preserves, or soap, or some other luxury in short supply these days. She won the contest again. She always does. Her version of Utopia is always the best.

Around us, everyone is clearing out. Ma kneels down, and I crawl up on her back. We head home with Graham and his Pa walking beside us.

They say goodnight when we reach the fork in the dirt road.

Ma ain't really my mother; she's my grandmother. But my mother is gone. She left on a mission to the incorporated territory two years ago and hasn't come back.

Everyone calls my grandmother Ma, so I do too. Big Ma was her mother. We call my mother Little Mother, on account of her having me when she was so young—sixteen.

Things have changed a lot in the generation since the incorporation.

Ma had Little Mother when she was 31. Now, cause of the situation with the food supply, and the ongoing skirmishes with the Kyintans and the drug cartels, women are encouraged to birth early. The babies are healthier and have a better chance at life.

Ma was born down south. She said it made her physically ache to leave her homeland. Like the deepest part of her soul was being wrenched away with every step north she took. She gets real sad when she tells me this, like the wound is fresh, even though it's been nigh on thirty years.

Little Mother and me was born right here in the Free Territories. Ma says that's life going on as life does.

Often enough, Ma reminisces about the day I was born. It makes me feel real good, not just like I'm loved, but like I'm wanted. It almost makes up for Little Mother leaving me behind.

"When you was born," Ma says, "you pressed your fists

tight up against your chest, with your fingers curled so they hid inside. And then you folded your knees up to your belly, so we had to hunt for your toes."

After she says that, I always clench my fingers around my thumbs, and press my knuckles against my heart. It's kinda sign language for, "You and Little Mother is precious to me, too." Although more and more I'm not right sure Little Mother is precious to me.

Every few months, a grime-encrusted circuit rider reaches our settlement with bleak news and a handful of letters. I always hope there's one for me. There never is. I never say nothing, just stuff the sadness down into the black hole Little Mother left inside me. Every day, it grows a little bigger.

"And your skin was so pale—unusual for a newborn, cause most times their skin is a patch of red blotches." Ma taps her lip. "But not yours. No, you looked just like a magnolia bud from the first moment. Those trees are ancient, and their buds are so tough." She crouches down to run two weathered fingers real soft against my cheek.

"But their petals are creamy to the touch." Then she gives me a whopping smile. "Hain't ever been able to get one of those trees to grow up here, but I got my Mags."

She grabs me and squeezes me so tight it feels like I'm gonna break in two. I squeal and squirm as she plasters me with sloppy kisses.

That's our ritual.

And my name is Magnolia, but everyone calls me Mags.

Graham

I reckon I've loved Magnolia from the moment I saw her. Except I cain't rightly remember when that was on account of I was so young. Something about her dark green eyes, pale white skin, and cocoa-brown hair draws me to her. She's the shade under a tree on a high summer day when your face gets burnt just crossing the yard. I'm the best friend she's got. Though I confess that's not saying much, since I'm the only friend she's got. Mags ain't really friendly. I don't blame her. A lot of folks think she's lazy on account of she can stay quiet and still for so long. But she ain't lazy, she's just real thoughtful and deep.

One morning, when Mags and I are eight years old, we sneak away from the settlement. She likes getting away from folks. It calms her almost as much as the quiet of dawn—Mags never misses a sunrise.

After we go a good distance, we reach an open field and stretch out in the long grass. Even though neither of us says much, it's nice being with her. It always is.

After we've been lying there for almost half the day, I peek sideways.

She feels my eyes on her and twists to her side. A smile softens her face, and those big green eyes sparkle.

Even though Mags is prickly, there's something about her that's hard not to notice. From time to time I catch other boys in our settlement staring at her. It makes me feel protective. Maybe jealous, too. Today I want to know if she feels what I do: We got a connection that others don't share. But I ain't sure how to ask her. Maybe roundabout. "I know I'm not the best looking boy in our settlement," I begin.

She props herself up on her elbow, like she's real interested in what I got to say.

So I go on. "I'm also not the smartest or the strongest." My heart sinks a touch when she doesn't argue my points, but I'm halfway across the river. If I don't keep swimming, I'm gonna get swept away in the current. My gaze settles on my long legs. "But I reckon, one day, I'm gonna be the tallest."

A giggle spills outta her mouth. The tight band squeezing my chest loosens. She rolls onto her back. We stare at the clouds floating by. I try to figure out what to say next, but I'm stumped.

"Graham, none of that other stuff matters."

Her announcement stops my mind's churning for more words.

"Cause you got a right true heart, and a right true heart is the thing in this world that's got the most value."

I relax back in the grass. The rest of the afternoon we don't talk much. We don't need to.

Pa says being quiet and comfortable in another person's presence is proof of companionability.

Mags and I is definitely companionable.

Mags

"Hush, Mags." Ma wraps her arm around my shoulders and pulls me to her. "Don't say nothing." She crouches down until her chin rests on the top of my head. My heart thumps in my chest, a biological GPS thudding a relentless, We right here. I'm sure whoever or whatever is out there can hear it.

Over my deafening pulse, I hear Ma sniff.

Gasoline.

Then I hear the glug-glug-glug of the fuel being poured. Ma's arm eases off my shoulder. I glance sideways and see her rise and point toward the brush.

She mouths, "River," and pushes the air with her hands.

I don't wait. I turn and run. I cain't hear her tread, but Ma can move through her forest quieter than anyone or anything that lives there.

I reach the steep bank and slip into the water as noiselessly as possible When I surface, Ma don't. "Ma?" At first, I just whisper and swish my hands beneath the water, searching. She was right behind me. "Ma, where are you?" My heart cracks open like an egg. Black yolk spills out. My voice pitches higher as I grope the river. My hands remain stubbornly empty, and my thrashing sounds like it's being blasted through some rickety PA system. I need to calm down. Ma won't approve if I drown.

Maybe she's done some scouting and will join me quick. I stretch my toes, but still cain't touch bottom. I peer behind me. I'm treading water in the river's deep center. I kick out my legs, soft and quiet, and butterfly to the river's south bank.

When I can curl my toes in the muddy sand, I crouch, willing Ma to join me.

But she don't.

The first explosion cracks my ears hard. Putrid brown-black flames crest in the sky. Ma's forest pops and crackles—a mountain-size version of a campfire.

For a second I hearken back to sitting around the warm, orange glow at night.

But this morning, a chorus of sadness wails from the flames like a mighty ghost. A supernatural terror sweeps through me is the best way I can explain it. There's no words, and there's no tune, only a song of despair raining down upon me like a storm.

I'm never gonna feel joy around a fire again.

An even bigger explosion rocks the ground.

Heat blankets my face. I'm sure my skin is on fire, but it's only my heart, scorching with terror for Ma.

The high-pitched squeal of pigs and the smell of their burnt flesh add to the gruesome mix. Last week, three sows farrowed. Those poor piglets.

I smash the backs of my hands against the river's surface, my legs paralyzed. If Ma walks outta that inferno —crisp like the bark on the black walnut trees—she's gonna need help—medicine and bandages and such. And she'll wanna see me first thing. She'll wanna know I'm safe.

Ma's whip smart. Maybe she ain't on fire.

Then I remember the irrigation ditches. I pull myself outta the river and tear alongside the water in the direction of the flames. I get a bad stitch in my side and have to push my hand against my abdomen so I can keep up my pace. When I see the pulleys and chains that operate the gate to the reservoir, hope explodes in my head. I'm gonna save Ma, and her forest, and them pigs. She's gonna be so damned proud. Probly tell stories round the campfire for years about how her little Mags was a hero the day the incorporators dared set fire to her woods.

Ma's outraged voice fills my head: Can you believe it? They went after my trees!

But the rusted metal of the pulleys ain't easy to yank. In a part of the country where rain is plentiful, the mechanism is a back-up measure, the least used part of the settlement's emergency relief program.

I grab the rusty links and pull with every ounce of my

body. Barely a creak. I step back five feet, ten feet, and give myself a running head start and leap. My chest slams against the stubborn chains, and for an instant, the smell of iron hits my senses. The lever shifts about an inch-and-a-half. I repeat launching myself at the metal ropes again and again. Finally, the lever swings back, and the gate rises enough for stagnant water to rush down the gullies Ma ordered dug years ago, before I was even born. Maybe even before Little Mother was born.

I cry out, watching the water gush toward the fire. To stay clear of the ever-thickening smoke, I get down on my belly and wiggle alongside the growing stream. I head straight for the destruction.

Shouts ring out. The rescue folks from our settlement is on their way. But I ain't about to wait for em.

I gotta find Ma right now.

Soot and ash thicken the air. Even down low, I can hardly breathe or see. I keep twisting my hips, pushing off with my toes, and clawing with my fingers, certain any minute I'll see Ma emerge from the black haze, like some superhero we watch in the movies on Friday nights in the community building. Ma's style is military with guns and knives and magazines crisscrossed over her chest. She wears boots and camouflage, and winds her long gray hair in a single braid pinned tight at the nape of her neck. No jewelry or makeup. But she's the most beautiful woman in the settlement with her leaf-green eyes and bark-tanned skin. And she's supple, moving like a sapling swaying in the wind.

When the heat gets too much, I make myself stand. Giving no heed to safety, I race around the burn site, bug-eyed. I figure the arsonists have already fled, cause I don't come across no one, even when I scream Ma's name until my lungs hurt and my throat feels raw.

When I wake up in my own bed, Da's hovering over me. I struggle to raise my head. "How'd I get here?" Every word makes my throat bleed, at least that's what it feels like. I rub my neck although it don't soothe anything.

"The rescue found you, on fire with the delirium," he

says. "Old Man tried to give you some lemon balm to chew on, and you almost took his finger off."

I'm trying to piece together what happened before the world turned black. "Why ain't you at the shop?" Da is the village butcher.

"Need to watch over my little girl."

The softness in his voice sets me on edge. Da's a lot of things, tender ain't one of them. "Where's Ma?"

He pushes the hair from my forehead with rough fingers. "She's gone."

I'm having a baby and it's name is Dread. "Where?"

He turns his face up to the tin ceiling.

Silent sobs rack my body. That baby I just had is wailing, and I don't think I'm gonna make it.

"Now, now, little girl."

I struggle to sit up. "I'm gonna be sick."

Da gets the bucket and rubs my back, but only a stream of white and yellow spittle chokes from my lips. I settle back down in bed.

"Let me get Franny," he says. "She can make you some

of her fine ginger tea. We need to start getting some nourishment back in ya."

I roll over and stare at the rough-hewn logs that make up the walls of our cabin. All I can think as I hear him shuffle across the dirt floor is that those logs is dead—just like the trees in Ma's forest, just like Ma and all her pigs. I cover my head with a quilt Big Ma made, and let the tears wash through me like a river.

I'm eleven years old.

Graham

Mags is different after Ma dies. Worse. She don't laugh and stalks off whenever someone tries to be funny. It earns her all kinds of new names: Grumpy Butt, Frowny Freak, Stick-in-the-Mudhole.

I run as much interference for her as I can, and she seems to appreciate it, but she seeks out my company less and less. I understand. The wound cuts to the roots of her, and it will take more than one season to heal.

One night me and Pa are eating dinner. I wait until

we're almost done before I bring up the topic weighing on my mind. "Have you heard, Mag's Da is writing laws now?"

"Ummhmm." Pa sops up the last bit of sausage grease with a heel of bread. "He ain't wasting no time. Giving speeches, too. 'It's morally wrong for a woman to go off on her own—and against her husband's approval—especially in these trying times.'" Pa snorts. "He always resented Little Mother's abandonment. He'd still be ordering her around if Ma hadn't encouraged her daughter's ambitions to preach."

"But why does he have to go and make 'spousal abandonment' a crime?" I ask.

"A weak man prefers controlling others to controlling himself. He wants this law passed so next time he marries his wife cain't leave him."

"He's not gonna give up on it. He's going after the votes."

"Franny gonna help him?" he asks.

"Pretty sure."

"That's unfortunate," Pa says. "Franny's got a way of wheedling and whining that makes folks say 'yes' just to shut her up."

"I know. And I'm worried about how it's all gonna affect Mags. She don't like Franny. As long as Ma was alive, Franny left Mags alone."

"Ma was tough. Her death—and Mag's unapologetic sadness about it—makes everyone in the settlement feel vulnerable. Like death might come for us all without a dark cloud warning or crack of thunder."

His words don't ease my mind in the least.

The day the law passes, the corners of Mags' lips bow down into an unyielding glower. "I'm never getting married," she says.

I don't doubt her for a minute. Mags don't lie. But my heart does ache, cause I've been dreaming about taking her for my bride for an awful long time.

two

Mags

It didn't happen like they thought it would. Not at first. They thought a big bang—a nuclear apocalypse, an orchestrated drone attack, or out-of-control Artificial Intelligence—would end the world as they knew it. But even the most evil people have a self-preservation instinct, so it wasn't the atom bomb that ended civilization, and no chemical or biological weapons was needed.

It was the gun-free zones and the whole country getting sick. The shootings in the schools and malls across the country always happened in gun-free zones. Though the state-run media never mentioned that, the shooters knew. Ma always said, If that had been advertised the way pharmaceuticals were, we'd be living in a different world. Then she'd snort in disgust. Ma hated pills. Some of the folks in our settlement used to swear by vitamins, but it's been over two decades since the Corporation annexed Imyrika, and whatever stash of pills we come across scavenging these days is long expired.

Ma believed in nature. Nature made us, not some damn machine or scientist, she'd huff at the council meetings. Mostly when she was demanding water rights for the forest farm. Folks listened to Ma, hung on her every word. She had a quality about her, quiet and strong, mighty and pure. And back then, everyone in the settlement was healthy—in their bodies, in their minds, and in their hearts.

Everything we ate, we grew or raised ourselves. And every time we sat down to eat, Ma would say, God bless fat. It's what feeds our brains and makes us smart.

Who was gonna argue with the underground videos of the incorporation still floating around? Videos of real people who looked like zombies. No, they didn't rock from side to side when they walked, and they didn't hold out their arms straight in front of em. Their arms are too damn weak to hold up, Ma would say. But their skin was pale and pocked. Doctors used to warn folks to stay outta the sun. And their eyes were glazed and faces expressionless. It's on account of the trash they fed em, Ma would say. And the propaganda they used to sell it—a food pyramid with fat a small speck at the pinnacle.

When over sixty percent of the population was overweight, clinically depressed, on welfare, and couldn't think straight anymore, they abolished the Right to Defense Act.

They starved their brains cause they couldn't take their guns away until they made em stupid, Ma would say. Not in a mean way, but in a definite way.

She had a ripe tart tongue, Ma did. Used to make me laugh and giggle, but I don't ever repeat the things she told me, cause I know most folks don't see the humor in it the way I do.

Ma loved the good Earth and everything on it, including the people.

She just wanted everything and everyone to grow up straight and true, cause she carried visions of Utopia in her head and in her heart. No matter what happened, you couldn't shake those visions from her. Like leaves on a rooted tree, her visions never fell away, no matter how strong the crosswinds blew.

Anyway, back then, the Kyintans weren't as stupid as the Imyrikans. They didn't risk coming until all the law-abiding citizens of Imyrika surrendered their guns and ammunition. The key distinction being law-abiding, Cause the criminals didn't queue up to surrender their arsenals, Ma would say if the subject ever came up.

Once everyone was chipped and registered—that took a while, government bureaucracy and all—the Kyintans arrived. Surgically orchestrated EMP events knocked out radar, cell phones, air towers—anything that might have seen em coming. The targets were meticulously chosen so folks could keep their TVs on.

Suburbia fell asleep on their Kyintan-manufactured sofas watching Crime Scene: Big City or The Confessions of a Werewolf while cargo planes full of Kyintan nationals landed in the parking lots of megastores. That next morning, everyone woke up with armed Kyintan soldiers at their front and back doors.

The traitors in the Imyrikan government, which included the president, his cabinet, the highest judges in the land, and the majority of the elected officials, had been flown to an undisclosed location that same night. Nobody ever heard from em again. Most folks think the Kyintans killed em, but nobody really cares. They sold us all out. There had been a handful of assassinations—coordinated precision strikes of powerful and loyal Imyrikans, but it was quick. A blink of a lazy eye, Ma said.

A new Imyrikan president was installed, a guy who'd lost in the last election, and key high-ranking military personnel were granted extensive powers. The former vice president sold the incorporation with a shit-eating grin and scripted commercials.

Property rights, laws, everything like that was abolished in 24 hours. The Kyintans moved into homes and made slaves of whoever lived there. Families of five or six Imyrikans would get a single bedroom for living quarters. The Kyintans dictated their days and nights.

No more evil capitalism.

The irony: The new world order was called the Corporation. They had the audacity to claim they'd abolished war. But that wasn't even close to the truth. The effects of incorporation were just the same as war, its application just more insidious.

A few pockets of resistance fought for a while in the East and Deep South, but everyone who craved freedom eventually fled north and then west.

Now the Northwest is a collection of about a thousand settlements known as the Free Territories. For a good long while, the Corporation and drug lords let us be. Then, we started sending out the missions.

Graham

Mags is angry her mother left her, more so now that Ma's gone. She don't like to talk much about it, but she don't let it go neither. She carries em both around like deadwood. Mags acts like she's real interested in history, but the only thing she really wants to understand is why Little Mother abandoned her for the mission.

"Why cain't she just preach here?" Mags asks me.

"Did you ever put that question to Ma?"

"No," she says.

"Why not?"

"I don't know."

"Maybe you should of asked her. Maybe she could of given you some peace about it," I say.

"What if she didn't know the answer? Have you ever thought about that?"

"Maybe Little Mother told Ma why she was leaving

before she left. Maybe Ma was gonna talk to you about it when you got older. Maybe she just didn't get the chance." I stop myself. Bringing up Ma's death is a mistake.

"Look, if someone asked Da about why I do what I do, you think he could give a straight answer? No! He don't know me. Even though he's my flesh and blood, he don't know what's in my heart!" She's pounding her chest. "He cain't answer the truth for me. No one can answer the truth for no one else." Her gaze turns inward. "One day, though, I'm gonna ask Little Mother myself." Then she turns all broody.

So I let her be.

She starts drifting off more and more on her own.

It has me worried until, one day, I make a discovery when I'm in the vegetable garden hoeing. I'm going just as hard as I can, so I won't have to think about how much I miss her. Everyone else has left for dinner. My hands and boots are filthy with dirt, and the evening ain't cooling down in the least. I pull my socks and boots off and run my hands and feet through the garden hose. As soon as my naked feet are planted flat against the ground, I get a strange sensation in my soles. Then it kinda travels up my calves, past the backs of my knees and my legs, and it doesn't stop until it runs all the way through my chest and up to the top of my head.

A buzz in my eyes draws my gaze west. I start walking in that direction.

The buzz doesn't grow stronger as I go along, nor does it lessen. It just stays real steady. I walk four miles, and it's dark by the time I come across Magnolia, stretched out by the river on her belly, deep in sleep.

I cain't just leave her there alone, even though she knows these lands better than anyone. I worry about attacks by the Corporation and the drug cartels. She's carrying a pistol, but she's far too vulnerable this far from the settlement.

I crouch down next to her and gently wake her.

"How'd you find me?" she asks.

"Just out for a walk and stumbled across you is all."

Her ruffled expression makes it clear she doesn't believe me. Nevertheless, she walks with me back to the settlement that night.

I do lots more experiments with the buzz in my head. Now, I almost look forward to when she goes off so I can see if I can find her. She's easiest to feel when she's connected to the ground too, running barefoot or digging in the dirt, but the more I practice, standing with the soles of my feet touching the earth directly, I can sense her anywhere, no matter where she is. I'll never admit this truth to her—or anyone else. But I use it to look after her and make sure she's always safe.

There's something between me, Mags, and the Earth that binds us together. So, the way I figure, even if she won't marry me, Mags is my girl.

When we haven't talked for a few days, I'll slip my boots and socks off, spread my toes and dig em into the earth, and wait. Shortly, that buzz pulls my eyes in a certain direction, and if I follow that invisible yank, I always find her.

Every single time.

It's kinda like magic and keeps me from worrying too much about her when she disappears, as she's inclined to do.

three

Mags

The rows of scraggly seedlings stir a familiar rage in my belly. I'm fourteen and it's the third spring since Ma died. This is it. I don't have no more black walnuts left. The first summer after the fire, I collected two bushels of seeds in their hard shells and portioned em out to last several planting seasons. But the fire was too hot. Even after three years, nothing but weeds and plants I cain't name will grow in the burn site.

In my heart, I finally understand: Ma's forest farm ain't

never gonna be resurrected. I water the meager sprouts outta habit as the black pit of hopelessness wells up within me. I could water em with my tears.

Life without Ma is a loneliness I couldn't have imagined. Determination to regrow her forest has been my way of hanging on, but I'm gonna succumb to the grief madness if I don't let her go.

When my water bucket is empty, I collapse to my hands and knees and poke my fingers as deep into the dirt as they will go. I mumble a rambling goodbye that a preacher might dub a prayer. Worn down by the sad truth I don't wanna claim, I roll to my side and press my fevered cheek against the ground.

I don't know how long I lie there, whimpering and moaning, wrapping my arms around myself until my last tear is wrung outta me.

When I get up, I swear Ma's spirit caresses my grimy forehead, though anyone else would believe it was just the wind. Ma has heard my sorrow and is urging me on: Yes, it's time to let my farm go. Time to move on. But I'll always live in your heart, little girl. Just like you'll always live in mine.

Those thoughts perk me up a bit cause I know they're true.

I look around, a little surprised Graham hasn't found me. These days, he has an uncanny knack for discovering my hideouts. It kinda soothes me and gets me rattled at the same time.

I roll over and stare into the sky. It ain't that late after all. A lot of daylight remains. Graham doesn't skip school like me, that's why he hasn't come yet.

My outburst has cleansed me as much as it has wore me out.

Tired as I am, I also feel light, like a wind rustles through me, shaking up my thoughts and turning em to the future. For the first time in a long time, I don't wanna lie on the ground imagining I can remain still for eternity —or until Graham comes to fetch me. I wanna move. Walk fast and hard.

I wanna reconnect with the world, but I wanna do it on

my own terms and for my own purposes.

Back at the settlement, I follow the shadows along the backs of the new concrete buildings. I don't wanna be called out for skipping school, especially not today with all my new feelings making me determined. I scan the empty, dusty lane before I emerge from the shade and tear across the open space.

With my head down, I run smack into Franny.

"Shouldn't you be in school, little girl?"

What's she doing here? Spying on me or something? "I ain't your little girl," I snarl.

"You better watch that mouth of yours."

"Be hard to do."

"What'd you say?"

I raise my head. Her muddy-colored eyes squint with contempt, like she's got some kinda right to judge me. I wanna kick her so hard, looking at me like that. If Ma were still alive, she wouldn't dare. I stretch a little taller and give her my own stink eye. Ma wouldn't want me to bend to Franny's bullying. "Watching my mouth will be awful hard when I cain't see it."

A brittle laugh splits her skimpy lips. "Why, Mags, is that you trying to be funny, hon?" She reaches out to touch my hair, and I jerk away. Her whole face sours like she swallowed a lemon. On her, it's an improvement. "You know, little girl, you gotta learn to fit in better. The way you run off and keep to yourself, folks are starting to talk about you being not quite right in the head."

"My head ain't none of your business, Franny."

"Maybe it ain't my business, but it's the settlement's. These days, there ain't no room for freaks and weirdoes like your—" She stops.

I know she was fixing to say Ma, and it makes me so furious, I bust out with my finger up in her face. "You wanna know what everyone's talking about, Franny?" With every word, I take a step forward and she takes a step back. "They're talking about you shamelessly chasing my Da."

She snorts. "You don't understand nothing, little girl. Your mother abandoned him and you."

My crimson rage colors everything I see, but Franny ain't done. Cause Franny's never done.

"Your mother's never coming back, and your Da needs a wife who won't run off to save a planet that ain't worth the trouble."

I spit on her. I cain't help myself.

She whips out her hand and cracks my face with her palm.

We freeze, breathing hard and staring each other down.

"You can be all out mad at me as you want, but your Da don't like you skipping school. He told me so."

The tone of her voice is gloating, like winning Da's pathetic confidence is some kinda all-important prize. "I ain't gotta listen to you. You ain't my mother. You ain't my blood. You ain't even my friend. So get outta my way, and let me pass."

She steps aside, but I can feel her glare on me all the way to the front porch of our new home. My whole body's quivering and my cheek still stings.

After kicking off my muddy shoes and setting my

watering pail beside em, I slip inside. I tell myself no one's gonna listen to anything Franny says about me, but she's planted a seed that's already taken root.

What if they do?

The house's interior is dark and quiet. We keep the shades pulled during the day to keep things cool. Mostly it works. But not now. After running five miles in the heat of the day, and facing Franny head-on like I just done, it's hard to cool down.

Sweat is pouring from my brow, and my heart beats like a drum. I wave the thin cloth of my shirt in the still air with one hand and fan my face with the other as I head toward the computer.

Ma didn't truck with technology, but I love lots of things about it—the internet being number one. Of late, I've been spending my scraps of free time scanning for stories about Little Mother. I had no news of her until the settlement bought a shipment of computers and hooked us up last year. Now, I know there's an entire underground network devoted to her gospel of the Union of Nature and Man. Studying the articles, photos, and videos of her preaching will be my purpose from this day on.

I check the light spilling around the curtains. Da won't be home for a few more hours. My heart races as I loosen the floorboard and take out the small, smudged stack of notes I've begun to collect. If my dream of regrowing Ma's trees is dead, my dream of finding Little Mother is mewling like a half-starved cat.

Ma would of said that's the way of things, Life moves forward, and it don't stop just cause we stand still and stare behind us.

I sort through the few slips of paper—accounts I've recorded of Little Mother being sighted. I'll need more if I'm ever gonna catch up to her.

One thing's for sure, I ain't sticking around for Da and Franny's wedding.

Graham

Mags takes a turn for the better when she stops going to

the burn site. She don't exactly become lighthearted, but her eyes spark, and on occasion she laughs out loud or says something funny. When she does that, I think it surprises her as much as it does everyone else. Although she still misses lots of school, she gets on better with folks. Well, as better as Mags can.

Mags exists at the center of an invisible perimeter and others are not welcome in her private space.

By the time she's done with trying to regrow Ma's walnut trees and failed, everyone in the settlement has gotten used to Mags not being around much. The council never chides her absences from school. They left her to her own devices long ago, first from sympathy and pity, then just cause she slipped their minds. Plus, Ma casts a long shadow, even in death. And like Ma, her granddaughter can be difficult. None of the teachers want to take on the battle of her delinquency.

I don't know what Mags does when she ain't in school. She never volunteers and I never ask. Asking Mags too many questions just makes her clam up. I reckon if she ever wants to tell me, she will. And since I wear my boots to school, I never seek her out during those hours—only when I'm done with my homework and chores.

One thing is for sure, the world, the Free Territories, and the settlement continue to change a lot around us. And Mags' Da and his new girlfriend, Franny, always seem to be in the middle of the shit storm.

I don't much like their methods of sowing dissatisfaction and strife, but I cain't deny their effectiveness. It's the internet reports about Little Mother and how she's become an evangelist for the Union of Nature and Man that gets Da all lit up sometimes.

You can watch videos of Little Mother preaching, and when the cameras pan the crowds, you can see how the people is won over and moved. She looks a lot like Mags. And a little bit more like Ma, now that she's getting older. But she's a powerful speaker, and more folks have started migrating to the wilderness, creating new communities that don't eschew technology, but don't hold with the subjugation of nature either.

It's a kinda beautiful doctrine that appeals to something deep within me. I have a dream one night that Mags and me are traveling south. It's a good dream, but a strange one. I haven't heard of anyone leaving the Free Territories in years. There's too much unrest beyond our borders, and it's just too dangerous. But it's hard for me to imagine Mags doesn't ever wanna see her mother again.

"Did you see the latest video of Little Mother? The one with the magnolia tree in the background?" I ask her one day, real casual.

"Uh-huh."

"What do you think?"

She shrugs.

"Ain't that tree your namesake?" I ask.

"Uh-huh."

"Do you think you'll ever see her again?"

"Now that she's famous, Little Mother's never coming back here, pretty sure," she whispers, but she stares at the ground. Mags will look you straight in the eye, and make you feel like your insides are naked before her, but not this afternoon. It gives me an inkling she's hiding something.

"Reckon she's heard about Da and Franny?" I wonder out loud.

Mags' cheeks pink. "I reckon she don't care!"

Ouch. It's been awhile since Mags has snapped so hard. "Probly not."

"Why you so all curious about Little Mother all of a sudden?" Mags asks.

"I kinda like what she preaches."

"You do?"

"It makes a lot of sense to me, living in harmony with nature, not trying to dominate it, and not trying to pretend like we're gods who can do better."

Mags nods. "Me, too."

I feel real close to her in that moment. So close, I yearn to lean in and hug her to me. But I have no doubt, if I try to touch her, she'll bolt. So I keep my hands to myself.

The Tree Hugger

I never imagine she'll try to find Little Mother on her own. Why would I? Courtesy of the Kyintans, a desert of concrete and steel exists between Mags and her mom. A desert I never think Mags would dare cross alone.

Mags

"You gotta stop skipping school," Da says.

"And why is that?" I ask, as if I care about his answer.

"Cause what young man is gonna wanna stupid wife?"

"If breeding's all that matters, why's he gonna care if I'm dumb?"

Da sighs. "Mags, we're not aiming to raise a bunch of useless book readers. The revised curriculum focuses on skills you'll need when you have your own family."

"I'd rather be a useless book reader."

Da frowns. He ain't the butcher anymore. He's the assistant settlement officer, with ambitions to be the settlement officer in the next election.

"How was the council meeting today?" I ask him. The less we talk about me the better.

"The marriage and breeding ordinance passed with zero dissenting votes."

The target of the MBO is kids my age, those fixing to turn fifteen. The Free Territories have managed to maintain their borders, despite constant military strikes by the Corporation, and the drug cartels attempts at land grabbing, but it's no secret our population is dwindling, and births are at an all-time low.

My stomach churns. "That's disgusting." I let my metal spoon clang as loud as I can against the metal pot as I slop Da's stew into his bowl. I bite the inside of my cheek to stop my laughter when the soup bounces outta the bowl and spots his shirt.

"Mags!"

I make a fuss of offering him a paper towel. "Sorry, Da."

He grabs the wad of crumpled paper and glares. "How am I gonna become the settlement officer with you setting such a dismal example of womanhood?"

"I'm not a woman, I'm a teenager."

Both his fists hit the table. The dishes jump. His temper has gotten meaner with his growing ambitions. "Teenagers is a thing of the past. You're nigh fifteen, and you're an adult."

I squeeze into the rickety chair opposite him. "If I'm almost an adult, how come I cain't make up my own mind about what I wanna do with my life, and how I wanna live it?"

"Cause I'm your Da, and you're gonna do what I tell ya."

That's his answer for everything—do what I tell ya. Quite a thinker, my Da.

I stare into my bowl filled with so much more than physical nourishment. Thick with vegetables, chunks of bacon, and swirled with oil—it's a meal Ma would of been proud to eat, and I'm proud that I cooked it. The chipped stoneware, a bowl I salvaged, helps me remember her. So does the old straight-backed chair I'd refused to relinquish when we'd moved to our new home. They help remind me that I'm strong like she was. Not weak like Da.

And every passing day, with her farm dead, and the settlement's waning commitment to the things Ma revered, I'm determined to make my own way in life. Determined to be a real adult.

"Ma didn't believe in a man telling a woman what to do." My voice is quiet and shaky. I'm not even sure Da can hear me, but I keep on, blind rage hissing outta me like steam. "Not a husband telling a wife, and not a father telling a daughter."

Ma carried a picture of Little Mother's Da in a locket on a chain around her neck. She didn't talk much about him, other than to say he was the love of her life, and he died too soon. Sometimes I'd catch her staring at his photo with a wistful light in her green eyes. It always made me sad to see her like that.

"Do you miss him?" I would ask her.

"As much as I'm gonna miss you when my time comes." I knew she meant when she died.

"How you gonna miss me when you're dead, Ma?"

She would run her fingers through my hair and promise

me, "When our bodies give out, our spirits live on."

But I wasn't convinced. "How do you know that?"

She'd hug me tight. "I just do."

Now, I'm thinking what she told me might be true, cause it feels like she's standing right behind me, passing her backbone on to me.

"Dammit, Mags," Da says, "look where Ma's beliefs got her—dead!"

What a stupid thing for him to say. "I guess having Little Mother didn't keep her alive, then."

Da's eyes glint. "You need to shut your smart mouth and listen to me."

My appetite has evaporated. I shoot up from the table and knock over my chair. Wild urges surge through me. Everything about Da feels like chains. "No, Da. I don't gotta listen to you."

He stands up too. A good foot-and-a-half taller than me, his bulk threatens. He's yet to hit me, but I no longer doubt that he will. I've heard lots of whispers in the past six months about fathers hitting, beating, and even chaining their daughters up like dogs. I don't wanna believe em, but why would anyone make such stories up? So much for the Free Territories being free.

Da rounds the table. I force myself to stand straighter, press my arms flat against my sides. If he's gonna hit me, I'll take it full on.

"Did you hear me say the MBO passed?" His voice is steady, like he hasn't lost his mind with being greedy for power and control over other folk's lives.

"I heard you."

"It's the law now." He crosses his arms across his chest.

I guess he ain't gonna smack me for the first time, after all.

My pulse is flapping like the wings of a bird. "I'm just surprised the women voted for it, is all I'm saying." I tell myself backpedaling is the wise thing to do. Maybe that's not a lie.

"The women on the council understand how important breeding is. How many times do I have to tell you, Franny was the one who writ up the law in the first place."

Franny. The other night, I heard her tell Da I was too wild for a girl. They don't know I eavesdrop when they sit out on the front porch at night in the rockers, plotting settlement reforms.

During the day, Franny tries to hide her hate for me with sick-sweet smiles and nosy questions.

I don't try to hide my hate for Franny.

Rumors about her and Da have kicked up like dust in a windstorm, and the gossip grit sticks in my heart. Thoughts of Franny and Da sleeping together, under the same roof as me, leaves me feeling tainted. The only reason they ain't married yet is cause Da's still legally married to Little Mother. He's filed a petition of abandonment, and the waiting period will be finished in a few months.

But I'm gonna be gone by then.

Gotta be.

My gaze shifts to the loose floorboard Da has yet to discover. It's getting real close to time to execute my plan. "Whatever."

"Mags," Da says my name real quiet-like. It gets my attention. "I promised you to Graham."

"What?" I screech.

"He's fond of you, he's healthy, and he'll make you a good partner."

"Da!"

"I thought you liked him. I thought you'd be happy."

"I'm not even fifteen yet, and he's my best friend! I don't wanna—"

"You don't wanna what? Mating is the most natural thing in the world."

I shake my head and stalk out into the night.

I march for hours in the moonlight, searching for a tree that stands taller than me. It's hard to find one. All the trees near the settlement have been chopped down for one "good reason" or another. When I finally reach a sparse grove before dawn, I drop down into a cradle of knobby roots. I calculate the supplies I've stashed in the shed, where the settlement stores tools for the vegetable garden. They won't be enough to get me to Union Major, but they'll give me a good start. I can scavenge along the way. I'm one of the best scavengers in the settlement: silent, strong, and fast.

I try to imagine what my almost 3,000 mile journey is gonna be like, but it's impossible. Still, curled up against the tree, a wisp of hope flutters in my chest. If I leave real soon, I can make it to Union Major before the first autumn leaf falls. I try not to think about all the concrete I'll have to cross. I try to imagine seeing Little Mother for the first time in over a decade. I try to imagine Union Major, the first and largest union city, which internet reports say is growing every day.

Graham

"Mags, where are you?" I ask.

She stops pulling weeds in the row. "My mind just drifted, that was all."

I wanna ask her where her mind drifted to, but I don't. She's been extra skittish since the MBO passed. I've told her, I won't marry her against her will, but she's adamant the settlement won't give us no choice. It kinda hurts, her being so opposed to marrying me, but Mags ain't like other girls. So I tuck my pain away.

I get back to weeding. Sometimes that's the best way to be with Mags, turn your attention away from her and just get on with the business of being yourself.

Things are changing quick in the settlement. Folks have started brewing whiskey, and a lot of the men and young guys my age are starting to drink it. Big barrels are fermenting down at the burn site. Mags doesn't approve, but she don't voice her disapproval neither. These days, she's Miss Agreeable, everything's all right with her. It makes me jumpy, makes me fear a real bad storm is coming. I fear her tongue's scarred from biting it.

It's hot out, even though it's dusk. When I glance at her, a strand of thick, dark hair is stuck to the sweat on her cheek. I wanna wipe it away, but I force myself to ignore the impulse and turn back to my work. We're the only ones left in the fields.

"I know it's not your fault," she says all of a sudden.

I rock back on my heels and give her a good look.

"The MBO and everything. I know it's not your fault," she says.

"Mags—"

She holds up her hand. "Just hear me out, cause none of this is gonna be easy for me to say."

My heart is banging in my chest, but I keep still.

"If I was gonna get married, if that's what I wanted to do, you know, get married and have children, maybe I'd be all right with everything. But it's so hard to know for certain with the choice being ripped from me. That feels wrong to me. It feels wrong with every bone in my body and all the blood that runs through my veins. When I give it serious thought, I cain't hardly breathe! It's like I'm suffocating. So don't think it's you, Graham. Don't think I'm mad cause they promised me to you. That's not it. You've always been my friend. We always cared for each other, and you, well, you always did a lot more for me than I did for you."

Is that a tear rolling down her cheek?

"I just want you to know, I need you to know, I'm not one to spell everything out. But if it weren't for you, I don't think I could of survived Ma's death. So, thank you."

Her voice has gotten softer with every syllable, so I'm not exactly sure I'm hearing things right. But I'm straining and listening with everything I have.

"Thank you, Graham. Our friendship, it's been everything to me since Ma died."

That's a lot for Mags to give me. I try to let the meaning behind her words seep in—she hates the law, not me. She can get so worked up about it, sometimes it's hard to be sure.

"But I don't wanna be forced into being married and having kids."

"Course not, Mags. I understand."

"I think you do, Graham. I really think you do." She pats my arm and gets back to pulling weeds, even though the sun set while she opened her heart to me.

four

Panic mounting, I study my hand-drawn map. The river was supposed to lead me to an undeveloped valley between two mountains. I stare at the level, paved road before me and the steel buildings with reflective windows towering on either side. Both the street and its soulless sentinels look infinite from where I stand.

What did I do wrong, and how in the hell am I gonna fix it?

And why hasn't Graham showed up?

I couldn't ask him outright to abandon his Pa, but in my heart of hearts, I wanted him to come without my asking. The awareness kinda jolts me, and it's not a good kinda jolt. But I cain't afford to dwell on what kinda enormous mistake I might have made by not confiding in him now.

I turn my map around and around, mystified as to how I could of gotten things so messed up. If I backtrack—and the settlement catches up to me—no one needs to tell me I ain't gonna get no second chances with Franny and Da.

I squint into the twilight. The Corporation cemented entire cities. Uprooted anything and everything green. Up until now, I've only seen pictures on the internet. Standing at the edge of one, for real, I feel so mad. Betrayed.

Like my soul has been negated.

A horrible fear possesses my mind. What if there's no wilderness left? What if all the maps I found on the internet are outdated? I suck on a thick strand of hair, nursing on it like a kitten on its mother's teat. What if all the reports I read about the growing number of union believers and towns ain't even real? What if I dreamt em all up or something?

Dammit, no!

I shake my head convulsively. Hundreds of videos were posted on the underground layers of the internet over the past year alone. I'd watched em all before they were scrubbed.

Acres of trees planted in the wilderness—they're still being planted!—are finally growing into new forests. Not only that, but forest farms are being cultivated. And wherever that's happening, the population is healing, not just in their bodies, but also in their minds and hearts. The pockets of believers in Little Mother's gospel of the Union of Nature and Man are spreading across the entire continent: no more domination of anyone or anything.

I have to believe it.

I sniff the air but cain't smell a single plant ahead. The pack on my back has several more days' worth of food. If I'm strict with my rations, I can make it last maybe another week.

I try to recall the different maps I studied on the internet. The largest swathes of wilderness are to the north. So are the mountains. Mountains that will double the length of my trip. I need to reach Union Major before the first snow. I'll freeze to death if I get caught in the mountains during winter.

I jam my obviously wrong map back into my jeans pocket and angle south. There's gotta be at least a sliver of wilderness in that direction.

There's just gotta be.

The road remains eerily quiet. Not a person in sight and no sound except for my boot heels scuffing against the cement. The entire city is deserted, and the creep factor is off the charts. The farther I go, the more curiosity overtakes my fear. After jogging a couple miles, I get up my nerve to try one of the doors on one of the monstrous buildings. I pull on the handle, then shove hard against the hard glass. It don't budge either way. I push again, throwing my shoulder into it. Nothing. For a few blocks, I test every door I pass. They're all locked. Every one of em.

At one point, I venture into the middle of the street and spin in circles.

Where is everyone?

There ain't even cars or anything parked along the side of the road. Just the empty buildings with not one light turned on as far as I can see. I keep moving, telling myself this unexpected emptiness is better than unexpected armies.

By the end of the night, my heels ache and I'm certain my calf and thigh bones have splintered from pounding the pavement. It ain't the same as walking on dirt. I can walk the bare ground for days and it's like my feet and legs have springs, drawing energy from the earth.

Walking these dead streets is different. Not a good different.

Right before sunrise, I search for a sleeping place. The air has gotten warmer through the night. The day's gonna be a scorcher. I settle in a nook behind a gate and beneath a ledge. I doubt anyone can spot me in the shadows–if anyone's left in the city to look.

I doubt it.

I try to imagine what happened. Maybe it's a new city and they just ain't moved people in yet. Or maybe it's some kinda model city and no one was ever intended to live here. Seems like a colossal waste.

I tear off a handful of pemmican and chew slowly.

A few reports on the internet said the Kyintans had become as sickly on engineered food as the Imyrikans had on crap food. Trusting in their ability to improve on nature, the Kyintans had fed the population a highly controlled diet that consisted of pills and packages of nutritional syrup in seven flavors.

I didn't pay the reports much heed, cause they were just snippets that never garnered any comments or verification codes before they were scrubbed.

Now, I wonder, what if they were true?

Kinda good and bad news.

I stop nibbling on my pemmican. What if I cain't find anything to eat when I run outta food?

I've imagined getting tracked by the settlement, I've imagined being taken into custody by the Kyintans, and I've imagined getting lost in the wilderness, but I've never imagined starving to death on a deserted cement road.

I'd also come across a few reports about encroaching drug cartels that had left large pockets of the Corporation lawless and unpopulated. I didn't pay em much heed either. Maybe I should of.

I fold my knees up until they reach my chest.

When Ma died, I felt completely alone in the world. If it hadn't been for Graham, and his silent, unwavering friendship, I would of never survived. I try not to think about how he must feel, knowing I left him without a thought or word of goodbye.

It's hard to convince myself I hain't cut him deep, like Little Mother cut me.

I punch my backpack into a pillow. It's too late for these kinda questions. I need to focus on where I'm going, not where I've been.

But another monstrous black hole sucks up my heart,

leaving behind a world of hurt.

Closing my eyes and imagining myself cradled in an enormous oak, while Ma sings me a lullaby, is the only way I can tolerate the ache until I fall asleep.

Graham

Mags shies away from me in the days following her unexpected disclosure. I don't worry over much. She let me pass through the psychic rings that keep her safe, and now, she needs to push me back out. Moved by her gratitude, which has remained unspoken for years, I'm content to let her have some space. But right away, I go to work on Pa.

Is there some way to strike down the MBO?

Pa's not optimistic, but after days full of school and chores, I spend long nights discussing the possibilities with him. We decide to put out some quiet feelers. Is anyone else disgruntled with Da and Franny's high-handed jamming the law through in the first place?

The morning I plan to begin my survey, I decide to

check on Mags first. I hain't seen her in three or four days, which is unusual. But I've been so focused on the MBO, and it has felt like she's been right beside me, encouraging me on.

It's right before dawn when I slip outta the house barefoot. I face the rising sun with the soles of my feet pressed against a strip of grass, the only one in our yard, and wait for the buzz.

When it doesn't come right away, my heart gins up in my chest. But I stay still. Finally, it twinkles. But it's so damn faint. And to the east. Mags never goes east. The borders of the Free Territories are east. The Corporation is east.

I shake my head and rub the back of my neck. I swing my arms around and jump up and down. Something has gone wrong with our connection and I curse myself for letting so many days pass since I last checked on her.

When my blood is awake and running through my veins, I make myself stand real straight and real tall. The exact same thing happens again. It takes a long time to make the connection, it's coming from the east, and it's feeble, more feeble than it's ever been. I leap up the porch steps and yell for Pa. "Something's wrong with Mags!"

"Whoa! Whoa, boy!" Pa has started fixing breakfast while I've been outside. "What are you talking about?"

"I don't have time to explain, Pa, but something real bad is wrong with her."

He takes my measure. "All right, then. You go on and do what you gotta do. But how do you know she's not at home with her Da, safe in bed?"

Mags loves the dawn. She never misses it as far as I know. She likes to be outside and feel the start of a new day on her skin and in her bones. She should of been outside with her own feet or knees or palms pressed against the ground when the sun rose, and the connection between us should be real strong. But even if she'd just slept in, and was safe in her bed in her Da's home, I'd feel her better. And the buzz would be coming from the southwest—not east! But I cain't explain all this to Pa.

A crushing feeling is building in my chest. If I don't get

a move on soon, I'm gonna lose her forever. I've never been more sure about anything in my life. "She's gone," I tell Pa. "I just know."

He doesn't question me and tries to help me think straight as I grab a pack and start throwing stuff in: dehydrated food, water packs, a good switchblade, a handful of flares, rope, and a couple cases of bullets for my pistol.

He hands me a couple lighters and a wad of old currency. Some folks still use it for trade. "Have any idea how long you'll be gone?"

"No, Pa, I don't."

Pa loved my mother with everything in his heart. Though he misses her, he always made it clear their love had left him fulfilled in a way nothing else ever could. "All right, then. Go on and bring your Mags back."

"Sure, Pa."

But the wheels of my mind are spinning. If Mags has run away, purposeful, mad dogs won't be able to drag her back to the settlement.

I hug my Pa real hard.

I think we both know we might never see each other again.

Mags

It's three nights of walking with my legs and knees and ankles aching a little more each day before I hit the stink.

It's faint at first, then the wind shifts and I'm gagging. If my stomach wasn't empty, I'm sure I'd be on my knees, painting the pavement with its contents. But there's nothing left in it, not even for sickness. Only a few drops of water are left in my canteen.

I'm gonna be crawling and hallucinating before long.

I spin on my heels. I'm still traveling due east.

Not much has changed around me. I'm still in a concrete jungle, surrounded by vacant skyscrapers. The only thing I know to do is keep moving forward.

Water, food, dirt has to exist somewhere, don't it?

I'm so exhausted. I sleep longer into each night and halt

my marches well before sunrise. I no longer search for hiding places, just collapse on a metal bench or against a curb. When I hear the chik-chik-chik overhead, I'm convinced I'm dreaming, but I raise my head to look up anyway.

A damned helicopter.

I follow it with my eyes. Someone else in this godforsaken cement shithole is alive.

Hope flushes through me. I unscrew the top of my canteen and let the last drops trickle onto my tongue. Time to get moving.

I drag myself up with every ounce of will I have. By the time I hear the rush of water, I'm lurching, hanging on to handrails, limping along the backsides of benches, and slamming into buildings. I cut through the alley between two skyscrapers and fall down on my knees.

Water rushes from a man-made dam. It pours into a giant reservoir, and in the distance, out into a cement spillway.

Copters circle overhead, but I don't care whether they

spot me anymore. I lie down on the sidewalk. Tonight, I'm gonna find a way down there to drink my fill.

By the time I wake up, the helicopters are gone, the sky is empty. I crawl toward the sound of the waterfall. When I reach a round bridge, I peer down. On the far side is five miles of steps, more or less. Would I survive if I just threw myself off?

I make myself cross the narrow walkway and start sliding down on my butt, step-by-step. But when I'm about two-thirds of the way down, I just don't have any energy left. I decide it's safe enough to tumble over the edge.

Before I do, I think of Graham and Ma and Little Mother. I allow myself to wonder what kinda life Graham and I might've had together if I hadn't run away. It's a fleeting glimpse into a future that will never exist before I fling myself off the stairs.

It's easy to surrender as my body plummets.

When I slam into the water, for a second, I don't even respond, just let my body descend deeper, deeper,

deeper. But at some point, the scrap of life that still exists within me makes me piston my arms and legs. Right before it feels like my lungs are gonna explode, my body rockets up. It shoots up forever, and I fear I won't last until I break the water's surface, but then my head bobs up and I'm gulping air and water.

They're the most delicious thing I've ever tasted in my life.

When my lungs and thirst are sated, I let myself float, gazing up at the moon and stars. I'm gonna let the water carry me to wherever it's headed.

By late morning, my face is on fire. The sun's reflection on the water is too intense for me to float along all day. When I reach the paved bank, I'm disheartened. I sacrificed my backpack and everything in it when I hurled myself from the steps.

Last night, I didn't think it mattered. I didn't think I would survive. But this morning, the decision seems careless.

The channel's cement walls are slick with mold, and too

high for me to scale. I half-kick, half-swim in the direction of the current with one hand bracing myself against the wall.

Graham

I've lost my connection to Mags and I'm just about crazy. For the first time, I begin to understand what she must have suffered when Ma died and when Little Mother left her. It feels like somebody's gouged out my heart and left me living with a bloody, gaping hole in my chest.

The only thing I know to do is keep following the direction where I last sensed her signal. Sand dunes, trees, gullies, and rocky outcroppings challenge my will to make a straight line.

What if I've gotten completely turned around?

No, she was going due east. I check the sky—and so am I.

Mags

It's not until the next day that I spot the metal steps.

I haul myself up em. Even though I hain't eaten, the water's done me some good. Not even the sight of more endless cement can stop the hope building in my chest.

The water's flowing somewhere.

Graham

My eyes scan the horizon. As far as I can see, it's concrete and steel.

It's been days since the last time I've felt any connection with Mags, but the last time it came, it was still coming from the east. That has never changed.

Traveling east has brought me here, to the edge of this eerie city full of buildings and roads but no people.

Why would Mags come here?

I crouch down and press my palms to the ground.

Nothing.

I've got a hard decision to make.

I close my eyes and hold a picture of Mags in my mind. Even though I cain't feel the buzz of her, I know she's still alive. With each step of my journey, the conviction that I'd feel her death has grown in me. Maybe it's a mirage, something to cling to, to keep me sane. But it's all I've got. And if Mags is alive, I'm gonna find her.

The question is: Did she cross this boundary?

I take off my boots and strip off my filthy shirt and jeans. Buck naked, I flatten my back against the ground, my palms facedown, grinding the dirt at the edge of the paved city. Desperation keeps me glued to the earth. I don't wanna admit I cain't feel her, but I cain't.

Finally, I sit up.

If Mags has altered her direction, if she's remained in the Free Territories, I could feel her. But I cain't.

For some reckless reason, she entered this lifeless city. I'm sure of it.

I don't know what she was searching for, but I've gotta find her—or die trying.

Mags

It's seven more days until I see another living person. A

mangy Kyintan woman, who tries to club me over the head while I'm asleep. I roll over, jump up, and run. I don't wanna hurt no one, not even some crazy woman who wants to kill me. It's easy to outrun her cause she's in worse shape than I am. When I stop to catch my breath, I shudder, considering what she meant to do to me. I hain't eaten for days either.

Every now and then, an airplane, not a chopper, flies overhead. I flatten myself against the high cement walls that line the channel. I don't slip back in the water cause I hain't seen any more metal steps. But small chutes of water feed the channel, and I take a drink from em with regularity, cupping the stream in my hand and gulping it down like it's milk.

I don't ever wanna get as thirsty as I was when I gave up on myself and slipped off the steps, ever again.

Graham

On the seventh day, I hear jet engines. They're coming from the north side of the city and sound like they're headed straight toward me. I move fast to hide in the shadow of a metal awning until the airplane crosses overhead. It's the first sign of life I've encountered since I entered this godforsaken steel and cement wasteland. When silence fills the air again, I follow the plane's direction, more south than east. It's gotta be flying someplace where there are people. Mags must be there too.

Hope boosts my energy.

My hope grows stronger when I peer over the bridge and see thousands of gallons of water pouring into a man-made river. The water smells fresh, like it's safe to drink. Since I only have half a water pack left, I'm heartened. I tear across the bridge to the staircase on the other side. There are so many steps, and they climb so high, it'll be like going down the side of a mountain. But I don't hesitate. I've no doubt Mags came this way too.

Despite my enthusiasm, by the time I reach the bottom, I'm spent. My heels and knees and thighs feel like they're broken. I sit my butt down with my back leaning up against the stone wall. I need a few hours rest.

Before I let my eyes close, I observe my surroundings better. There's not much to see. Stone walls, yellowed with the passage of time, line the channel. They're as tall as the steps are high, so all I can see above me is sky.

There's only one way to go—forward. That gives me a kinda peace cause it's the only way Mags could of gone, too.

Mags

On the ninth day—I'm pretty sure it's the ninth day—I reach a cluster of shacks. Greenery stretches out behind em. If I'm not hallucinating, it's a line of trees. I'm certain I can smell em.

A man comes outta one of the buildings with a shotgun pointed at me. "Where you from?" he yells.

After a week of constant silence, his question sounds like a bomb going off in my head.

"Headed to the wilderness," I answer.

He doesn't lower the shotgun. I doubt he heard me, my

voice sounded faint, even to my ears. I wonder if I've forgotten how to talk. I raise my hands with my palms facing him.

"Hmmm." He don't seem happy to see me.

An older woman with a severe face comes outta the house behind him. They're both wearing what were probly once fine clothes, but now they're stained and worn. I imagine my outfit don't look so dandy either.

"Where is everyone?" I point my thumb back at the city, now some distance behind me.

He squints. "Is that where you came from?"

I nod.

I hear the bang of his gun before I feel my chest rip apart. Shock and pain consume me. I stumble forward and catch myself on my hands and knees. The man edges toward me, his gun still raised.

"Why'd you shoot?" I ask him.

"You don't look sick," he says.

It's getting harder for me to breathe. I press my hand to my chest. When I get a glimpse of my blood-soaked palm, my vision wavers, the world sways around me. "Please, help me. I'm dying."

He kicks me in the ribs and I collapse in the dirt. I run my hands across it, and though it feels like it's gonna kill me, I suck in a deep breath. God, it has been so long since I've felt or seen or touched the earth. I wanna consume it. Instead, I press my belly flat against it and rub my palms back and forth. I draw strength from it. It daubs my life force, keeps it from flowing outta me.

"You crazy?" he asks.

"What'd you shoot me for?"

"We can't let the sick ones pass," he says.

"I ain't sick," I gurgle.

"That's what they all say."

Hysteria wells in my chest. "Please, don't just leave me here to die."

"If you aren't infected, you'll live."

I black out.

Graham

The heat is sweltering. I'm bare chested with my shirt wrapped around my head. I soak the shirt in every chute that flows down into the channel. It offers a few minutes of relief. Enough to keep me moving.

five

Mags

The next day, I wake up handcuffed to a table in a bare room.

"She's up," a woman's voice crows.

I hear two different pairs of steps, one tentative, the other strong and clipped following behind it. Papery, smooth fingers brush my forehead. "She hasn't got a temperature. At least not to the touch."

The man who shot me enters my peripheral vision. He reaches out his hand.

I jerk away.

The woman leans over me and presses down on my arms.

"I'm a scientist with basic medical skills," he says. "Where are you from?"

There's at least one window in the room and the light filtering through it is bright. I squint, trying to get a better look at my captors while I calculate my response. They're not Kyintans. I doubt they're union either from what I can see of their clothes. Today, the man's got on a long-sleeved white coat, and it looks like the woman is wearing a long-sleeved dress. In this heat? I settle on being vague. "West."

"The Free Territories?" he asks.

I shrug. Reticence has served me well my entire life.

"What in the hell were you doing walking through a dead zone?" he asks.

Dead zone? That don't sound good. I flatten my lips into a defiant line.

"If we remove these bindings, will you stay put?"

"So you can shoot me again—and for no reason? Don't count on it."

"I had good reason for shooting you."

The woman rubs her hand up and down my forearm, kinda soothing, but I hold my limb real stiff. "These days we can't trust folks to tell the truth," she says.

"I guess shooting anyone that shows up on your doorstep is one way to rid yourself of potential liars," I say.

The man's all up in my face now, his eyes hard behind his thick, black framed spectacles. He grabs my chin. "This will go better for you if you cooperate."

His voice makes my skin crawl. I wanna spit but figure that might antagonize him. I just steel my eyes and glare right back.

"You traveling alone?" he asks.

"No, I'm leading a damned army," I mutter. "Do you see anyone else with me?"

He squeezes my jawbone.

I try to pull away.

The woman clamps her hands against my forehead. Her nails dig into my skin.

I bite my tongue so I won't give em the satisfaction of screaming.

"He just wants to examine you," she says.

"Maybe I don't wanna be examined."

They give each other a look over my head. The man dips his head. The woman shuffles off.

"You need to calm down," the man says.

Not a chance of that. My chest is bandaged and there's a dull throb beneath the gauze. I try to buck off the table, using my heels and shoulders. All it does is sharpen the pain in my chest. I manage to keep myself from crying like a two year old.

The man crosses his arms.

When the woman comes back, she's got a hypodermic needle in her hand. She gives it to the man.

"Hold her still," he says.

I do my best to make that impossible, but he still manages to poke me. I bellow so loud, I hope I bust his eardrums. A warm, thick feeling inches through me, like my blood is turning into maple syrup, but I don't black out or anything. I just feel like the world and everything in it, including me, has slowed down to an ant's pace.

"Now, let's try this again," he says.

He presses a small device into the hollow of my throat and several shallow needles prick my skin. When he's got it secure where he wants it, he pushes up on each of my eyelids. He takes a slim light from his breast pocket and pokes it up my nose and in my ears. Then he sticks his index finger in my mouth and rubs it along my gums. My mind is moving so slowly that by the time I think to bite down, his finger is already clear of the most effective weapon I've got. He examines my fingernails and then my toes. When he's done inspecting every inch of me except my privates, he collects the device pressed against my neck.

"Your pulse is high. That's to be expected because you're afraid. But your temperature is normal, and your blood sugar and all your other vitals are in optimal range."

Maybe we should throw a party.

"I need to ask you one more time." The man locks my eyes. "Why were you coming from a dead zone?"

I have no idea what he's talking about. "What's a dead zone?"

"You really don't know?"

The woman hurries from the room.

He pulls up the only chair in sight. "The Kyintans have authorized the use of biological weapons in ten cities over the past seven months. Millions are dead. The geographical sites of the attacks are dead zones."

He says it as if he's telling me he feels refreshed this morning cause he slept good last night. The information, delivered in such a cheery tone, triggers shockwaves in my mind. "But there were no bodies. Not one."

"They've all been burned."

The reality is overwhelming. "That's why the city was so —" I cain't think of a better word. "—clean?"

"Landis was the first target. Four reconstruction phases have already been completed."

"Reconstruction phases?"

"Phase one, clearance. All bodies are collected and transported to the incinerators. Phase two, demolition and hauling. All wreckage and debris is removed from the city. Phase three, decontamination. The environment is scrubbed to assure the contaminant has been eradicated. Phase four, rebuild. New roads and buildings are constructed. Phase five, screening. Viable repopulation candidates are interviewed and selected. Phase six, repopulation. The city is repopulated with a maximum of thirty humans per square mile."

"But there was no one in the entire city. No workers. Nothing."

"The construction corps has already been transported to the second attack site up the road, Enniston. It's all a grand experiment. Wipe out the vermin, clean up, rebuild, and renew."

"The vermin?"

"The useless people, the ones who don't contribute and are a drain on the rest of us."

I cain't have heard him right.

"And you're the best news that's come out of Landis in ages," he says.

Is that why he's all fired up, even though he's talking about a scale of mass murder beyond comprehension? "How's that?"

"We determined the pathogen's life span to be twelve hours outside the mammalian body. Unfortunately, incidents have been reported of animals becoming carriers. You're the first human to pass through the city without becoming infected."

"What about the people who burned the bodies?" I'm feeling woozy and clammy. I'm not sure if it's the drug he shot me up with earlier or the subject matter. Maybe a combination of both. "Or the construction corps?"

"The breathing devices in the latest generation of hazmat suits extend 120 minutes. Quite an improvement. Every year we seem to be able to increase the quality of air exchange and gain a few more minutes. The corps works in 90 minute shifts; the 30 minute cushion allows for transport to and from the command base."

"Are they done?" I ask.

"Excuse me?"

"Are they done using the biological weapons?"

He gets up from his chair and calls out the door. "Mother," he calls. "She needs to eat." He resettles in the chair. "I'm going to return to Landis and resume work in my lab. With the peace and quiet, I'll be able to work undisturbed while I create a new and improved strain of humanity."

The belief that man's fundamental purpose is to overcome the flaws of nature—including the flaws of humanity—is a Kyintan one. "But you look Imyrikan," I gasp.

"My only allegiance is to science. The Kyintans appreciate that."

"Kyintans lived in Landis too? The Corporation killed em right along with the Imyrikans?" I can hardly believe it.

"We ran tests. The results were conclusive. Regardless

of nationality, the population's DNA had deteriorated. Their bodies were inferior, their intellects even more inferior. They could hardly be classified as people."

My stomach heaves. "What happened to em?"

"Unioners blame a 100% synthetic diet and lack of exposure to vegetation, a disconnection from nature, if you will," he scoffs. "Every great discovery has been born of the knowledge gained from prior error."

I try to shrink myself, as if that might offer some protection against him learning that the leader of the union movement is my mom.

"The Kyintan government understands the true purpose of the collective."

I'd heard Ma rail about the collective once.

"People's lives are not their own. Nor is their labor, productivity, or offspring. Everything belongs to the government. Even the radical religious elements understand: Those in power are selected by a higher authority. I applaud the Kyintans rational objectivity in this regard. Every human is an opportunity to experiment, research, dissect, and improve."

Every cell in me recoils with horror. "Why cain't you just let people live?"

"We can't continue to allow inferiors to live off the productivity of superiors. It only breeds class warfare and foments dissent. No, we're going to create a new world order. Emphasis on order."

"Why ain't there any reports on the internet?"

"Project Renew is highly classified, and thankfully, what's left of the Kyintan government has managed to keep the news of our work from the rest of the world."

"Our?"

He stands up and bows. "Allow me to formally introduce myself. I'm Theodore Eliv. But you can call me God. I'm the creator of the Angel of Death."

I blink in shock. His claim ratchets my fear and revulsion off the charts. My mind pivots to a single goal. Escape. I'll need to get free of these restraints. Maybe if I act interested in what he's saying, he'll offer to loose my hands again. Now, I realize how dumb I was to mouth off in the first place. I swallow hard and try to make my voice sound reverent, interested. "Angel of Death?"

"The pathogen that allowed Project Renew to become something more than a lofty ideal that do-nothing scholars mentally masturbate over in ivory towers, yet never have the guts to realize."

He doesn't need any encouragement to keep talking.

"It's a bleeding disease. Once the pathogen enters the lungs, there's no antidote. Any wound much larger than six millimeters and the normal respiratory process allows the introduction of ample oxygen to activate the agent. You bleed out in days."

"But how do they release it?"

"They drop gas bombs laced with the toxin. Once the pathogen is airborne, inhaling a small dose achieves infection. It's quite potent. Saturation bombing follows, creating enough shrapnel to initiate the bleeding and assure death."

I cain't believe they've managed to keep news of this atrocity buried. The unioners, my mother, the Free

Territories, the world needs to be warned. Project Obliterate the Human Race has to be stopped.

Frustration overwhelms me. I'm awash with unfamiliar feelings of helplessness.

The old woman shuffles back into the room. She's carrying a mug with arthritic hands. Despite my emotional nausea, my physical hunger asserts itself.

"Will you behave if we remove your restraints?" Theodore asks.

I nod. But he looks more like a Teddy than a Theodore to me. That's not a compliment. His skin is pasty and his narrow face could of been squashed in a vertical vise.

He works on the leather straps. Getting my hands free is progress. I sit up slowly, wondering why he doesn't just shoot me up with some nutritional syrup. I take the mug and gaze at the contents. It's a gelatinous liquid.

"What is it?" I ask.

"A scientifically designed broth."

I hate that it smells delicious, and once I taste it, I gulp it down without pause. Teddy observes me with cold, calculating eyes.

The old woman takes the empty glass.

"Bring her another cup," he orders.

She exits the room like a ghost.

"When you finish eating, we'll need to check your wound."

"Did you use some special bullet to shoot me?"

"I used birdshot."

"Huh, that's why I'm not dead?"

"You're not dead because you've yet to meet the Angel of Death."

He says it like it's a joke and he expects me to laugh. The woman returns with another cup of broth. I mumble a thank you for good measure.

"Mother, meet Test Subject 122K."

His words chill me.

A slight smile creases the wrinkles that trough her cheeks. "Then I'm to assume she'll be returning to Landis with us?"

Teddy is a mama's boy. Why ain't I surprised?

"Yes. I'll notify my contact shortly to finalize the preparations for my lab and our living quarters."

My throat catches and my insides freeze. I feel like I've bolted down an entire frozen water pack. "You're gonna take me with you?"

"I'll need to run some analytics to verify, but preliminary observation and diagnostics indicate you're an exceptionally healthy female in the prime of her reproductive life cycle. With your high volume of viable eggs available for harvesting, I'll be able to proceed with my work."

The mug slips from my hands and shatters on the stone floor.

Teddy frowns. "Make a note, Mother. We'll need to test her motor skills for the final determination."

"I need to go to the bathroom," I say.

"I'll escort you." He loosens the leather straps around my ankles.

The drug that slowed me down is wearing off, but I resist the impulse to jam his cheekbone with my heel. I doubt I'll get more than one chance to get away from Teddy and his mother. I need to make it count.

Graham

The walls of the spillway are making a slope so gradual, the incline is barely perceptible to the naked eye. But the walls are definitely getting shorter. I pick up my pace.

Mags

After I go to the bathroom—it's an amazingly high tech sanitation system hidden by an askew door of faded wood —Teddy leads me to a room with dark curtains and a lumpy bed. Unlike the bathroom, the room's interior matches the dilapidated appearance of the rest of the house, though a stack of sleek, silver suitcases tower in the corner.

"Get some rest," he says, and stands there, staring, until I get into bed.

Beyond the old-wood doorframe, Teddy pushes some

buttons. Beep-beep-beep, a sliding panel whirs shut.

At least he's not some sexual pervert.

I slip back outta bed and examine the windows behind the curtains. They're made outta some kinda plastic. Probly bulletproof and escape proof. I tiptoe over to the suitcases. The first one is locked and heavy when I try to lift it. Since I don't wanna risk any bumps and crashes that will bring Teddy running, I crawl back in bed and study the water-stained ceiling.

Adrenaline pumps through my veins.

Graham

When I see the darker line against the early night sky, a horizon of land, I break into a run.

As soon as I leave the pavement, I throw myself on the ground, rubbing my hands in the dirt. The buzz of my connection with Mags fills me. She's close by.

Then I hold a clod of dirt up to my nose and smell blood. Mags' blood.

I keep myself flat on the ground.

A row of rundown shacks sits about a hundred yards ahead of me. They appear to be abandoned, but she's gotta be in one of em, the buzz is so strong.

Fear that she's bleeding out makes me wanna jump up and run, hollering her name, but a bleak feeling has taken hold of my spine. Something about what I'm seeing and sensing don't mesh.

Thankful for the cover of dark, and my dirt-covered clothes and skin that allow me to blend in with the ground, I stash my pistol behind my back in my belt and start pushing myself forward, keeping my belly flat against the earth and my ears perked. Nothing about what I'm seeing is helping me figure out what this place is or why Mags is here.

There are five cabins. I try to calculate how long I've been scraping along the ground. Ten, twenty minutes? And not a dog, cat, chicken, or child has made a sound. Course chickens roost when the sun sets, and it's almost dark. But what about other living things? It's too early for such unnatural silence, and the suffocating blanket of quiet ticks up my misgivings.

I angle toward the last house on my right. When I veer off, my connection with Mags weakens. Not much, but enough to make me certain that's not where she is. I pause. Still no sign of no one, but if someone peeked out any of the front windows, and I was spread out in the middle of the front yard, I'd be easy to pick out by someone with sharp eyes. And maybe by someone with not so sharp eyes, even though the light is getting dimmer every second. If I can make it to the yard's perimeter and get closer to the buildings where I'm outta line with the windows, I can maybe inch up around the foundations and find Mags without getting spotted. Of course, if she's holed up alone, my caution is overkill.

I hear something.

A whirring.

A metallic arm extends from the roof of the house second from the end of the row. The opposite end from the direction I'm headed. The polished sphere is totally outta place. It spins real slow, like it's trying to catch a signal.

To my way of thinking, this ain't good news and my caution is justified.

I worm my way faster across the ground without altering my course. When I reach the side of the house I'm aiming for, I'm rewarded with a solid wall, no windows. I shift up to the balls of my feet and monkey walk toward the back of the building. There's a door.

Sweat drips in my eyes. Night falling hasn't cooled the air much. Between the heat and the tension, buckets of perspiration are flooding from my pores. There are no windows on the back wall of the house either. When I test the doorknob, my hand is slick with sweat. I rub it against my pant leg and take a deep breath. Before I reach again, I dry my other hand, too, and take my gun from my belt. When I've got the safety off and the gun positioned, I curl my hands around the doorknob.

Damn. It's locked.

I spin on my heels, press my back against the wall, and try to calm my breathing. It's nigh impossible. My entire body is pulsing with apprehension and I cain't get it under control. Something ain't right, but underneath it all, I can still feel my connection with Mags. I focus on that and it settles me. I return to my crouch and head toward the next building.

Two more houses, two more locked doors, all the time my connection with Mags is growing stronger.

All right. That's good. She's alive and her heart is beating strong. That means, despite the smell of her blood in the dirt, she's not bleeding out.

A hip-high window runs almost the entire length of the fourth house, the one with the satellite dish. I shuffle beneath it, crouching. There's no back door on the fourth house, nor the fifth one neither. But my sense of Mags is strongest here. She's inside.

When I reach the corner of the building, I peer around the side. The moon is waning, so it doesn't offer much help. But by now, my eyes are well adjusted. Three black windows stare across the plains. One of em will take me to Mags.

This time I crawl.

She's behind the farthest window, the one closest to the front of the house. I sit with my back against the clapboard. I set down my gun and press my palms flat against the ground, drinking her in.

Mags

I sit upright in the bed.

Graham is close by.

I don't know why I think this, but I do. It's like my body is pulsing with the memory and hope of him. Maybe I'm dreaming. I ease outta bed and tiptoe to the locked door.

Everything is quiet.

I head to the window and push aside the curtain. Outside, the night is black. I stare into the void. My eyes adjust to the small amount of moonlight, but still I cain't see what I'm looking for.

One thing's for sure, I ain't asleep and this ain't a dream.

I wait, not sure what I'm waiting for.

No, I'm lying to myself. I'm waiting for Graham. He's here.

How could Graham be here? My heart races. He's found me, like he used to do.

I press my fingertips against the plastic window. I don't know if it's bulletproof, but it's definitely unbreakable. I slide my fingers along the seam, praying for a rift in the sealant. No such luck.

I keep waiting. It feels like forever, but I don't move.

Believing Graham is near makes me stronger.

six

Mags

When the first rays of daylight edge the sky with the light pink of rose petals, I'm still gazing out the window. It must be facing east, since I can see the sun directly. I take the sight of dawn as a good omen.

The tree line is south, and the cement gully that drained outta Landis is north. But all I can see from the window is an endless spread of dirt.

Where's Graham? His presence is strong, and I don't doubt it for a minute until a horrible thought ends my gaping. I stagger to the bed and flop down, a hope-broken rag doll. What if he's dead, and what if what I'm feeling is his spirit, hovering by my side?

I sob.

If that's what's happened, it's my fitting punishment for being so careless with his heart. Too late, I acknowledge my love for him and his gentle strength. What a fool I've been.

My drive to find Little Mother evaporates.

If Teddy wants to take me back to Landis and use me as a human pincushion, maybe I won't fight against him.

Graham

A rooster's crow pulls me outta my sleep. I must have dozed off. My torso's leaning all cockeyed, and my right shoulder and side of my neck are stiff. I straighten up.

The creak of a door hinge coming from the front of one of the houses puts my nerves on alert. I search for my gun, a few inches from my left hand.

Slow steps shuffle in my direction.

The Tree Hugger

I pull myself up to the balls of my feet and inch toward the back of the buildings.

As soon as I'm around the corner, I spy the small coop.

Damn. I wished I'd spotted it last night.

I straighten, press my back against the building, and ready my gun.

Someone's coming to collect the eggs. From the sound of the steps, it's someone I'm gonna be able to overpower without much trouble. As the uneven gait draws closer, I prepare to lunge.

I launch myself and we both sprawl on the ground. I keep a hold of my gun as I blanket the body beneath me. I press my legs and arms down hard to hold her still.

It's an old lady, dressed like she's going to church. "Please, don't kill me," she says.

"I don't wanna kill no one," I say softly in her ear. "Don't want no one to get hurt." But I don't let her up. "How many folks are inside?"

She don't answer.

"You got a girl with long dark hair and green eyes in

there?"

"I told Theodore she wasn't traveling alone. I guess he'll listen to me next time."

Her confirmation ignites my veins. "Is Theodore inside with Mags?" All peaceable notions have fled. If he's done anything to her, I'm gonna rip his arms off.

"Is that her name, Mags?"

"Yeah, that's her name and I'm gonna take her outta here."

"That might be difficult."

"Yeah, and why's that?"

"Because Theodore wired the installation unit last night and they're going to be here soon. So really," she says, "it doesn't matter how many people are inside. You and your girl aren't going to be able to fight off the small army that is on its way."

I shift and get to my knees while keeping a steel grip on the back of her neck. When I'm solid on my feet, I yank her up. She's light and doesn't offer much resistance. "Let's go talk to Theodore," I say.

She tries to stand firm, but only ends up stumbling. I press my gun to the back of her head. I ain't gonna shoot her, but I also ain't gonna volunteer that information.

When we get to the front door, a coded entry pad confounds me. "Enter the password."

She folds her arms.

"There's more than one way to do this." I drag her back off the squeaking old porch. When we're about two feet away, I wrap my arm around her chest and hold my gun to her head. More and more I'm convinced she and Theodore are the only ones who live in this strange government outpost, rigged to look like old, abandoned houses. But if anything she says is true, it won't be long before we have company. More company than I can handle.

I go with my instincts. "Theodore!" I have to holler his name about ten times before I hear the sound of more than one security panel slide open and the final whine of the dilapidated screen door.

The man stands on the porch with a shotgun.

"Mother!"

I should of guessed Theodore was her son. "I'll release your mother, if you release my Mags."

I can practically see the wheels turning inside his head. With his mother's body covering mine, there's no way he can get a shot at me. He narrows his eyes and lowers his gun. "Fine. Let her go."

"I wanna see Mags."

Theodore searches the sky.

"Now."

"Why don't you come inside? We can talk this out."

I laugh. I cain't help it. His tactics to delay until reinforcements arrive is too pitiful. "I'm not much of a talker."

"Mother, are you all right?" He's pacing the porch but keeping his shotgun down.

"Let him have the girl." Her voice is steel.

"Are you sure?" Theodore's voice is petulant.

"They won't get far."

He pulls a square cloth from his pocket and takes off his

glasses. When he starts wiping the lenses, I squeeze my arm tighter around his mother.

"It's all right, Teddy. Get the girl. I won't be upset." Her voice is softer this time, more of a mother coaxing an obstinate toddler.

"I should have believed you when you said she wasn't alone."

"I know, son. I forgive you."

He puts his glasses back on and shoves the napkin back into his pocket. After he retrieves his shotgun from where he leaned it against one of the sagging porch columns, he raises it and tears for me. I shoot him in the kneecap and he buckles. I'm a good shot.

He craters in the dirt.

His mother releases a bloodcurdling scream I fear has deafened me. She's sobbing hysterically, writhing, and clawing at me, ripping up the skin on my forearms with her fingernails. I manage to keep hold of her and lift her off the ground. I work my way to the door. Thank god, Teddy left it open. The entry hall is dark and smells like mold. I take a right into the first doorway and step into some kinda high-tech shiny cell full of screens and beeping equipment. A door on the other side of the room draws my attention.

The buzz is pumping in my brain. Mags.

I'm still hauling Teddy's mother and her feet are dragging the ground as I pull her toward that closed door. There's another keypad. Damn.

"Give me the code."

"You shot my son!"

"And I'll shoot you, maybe not to kill, but it will hurt like hell, if you don't tell me how to open this damned door."

Mags

My head pops up.

Gunshots.

I press my ear to the door.

Muffled thumps and voices are all I can hear. But one of the voices...

Graham?

I scream his name at the top of my lungs and bang on the door with my fists. I rear back and throw my shoulder into it. The pain radiates up my arm and I wince as it aggravates the injury in my chest. I spin around and slam my heel against the door. It gives a satisfying splinter but remains intact.

Dammit to hell!

I race to the corner of the room and shove the first suitcase on the floor. I test the clasp on the next one before pushing it from the stack. Every single one is locked. I find the one I can lift and head back to the door. Bracing myself, I prepare to bludgeon the wood with the metal satchel.

Just when I'm about to make the first swing, the door busts open.

Graham has got his arm around Teddy's mother, his gun pressed against her head.

"You little bitch," she says.

Her angry words hardly register. I'm shaking with relief

at the sight of Graham's earth-brown eyes and towering frame. "God, it's good to see you," I say.

"Mags." The break in his voice rocks my heart with powerful emotion. "Mags, we don't got much time. We gotta run. What happened to your chest?"

"It's nothing," I lie. Teddy may not have killed me, but his birdshot tore me up pretty good. The left side of my rib cage is aching worse with every passing hour.

"Get on some shoes quick," he says.

"They took em from me."

"Where are her damn shoes?" he yells at Teddy's mother.

"We burnt them. Burnt all her clothes to decrease the risk of contamination." Her voice is smug.

"Damn!" Graham yells.

My sentiments exactly.

"You have any boots?" he asks her.

"No."

"I can run barefoot," I assure him.

Doubt clouds his face.

The faint sound of choppers hits us.

"We don't gotta choice, Graham. We gotta get. Now."

Keeping a grip on the old woman, he moves aside to let me pass.

Teddy's halfway up the porch steps with his shotgun under his arm. I kick it out from beneath him with my bare foot. It flies into the dirt beyond his reach, but the pain is so bad, I'm afraid I broke at least a few of my toes. I'm limping when Teddy's hand snakes around my ankle and jerks hard. My balance is shot and my face is halfway to the ground when Graham catches my bicep. He's got long arms and sure fingers. When he slides his other arm behind my knees and lifts me up, hugging me close to his chest in one smooth motion, I swivel my head.

"Where's his mother?"

Graham practically leaps from the porch and breaks into a strong run. As tall and lanky as Graham is, he's never lacked for muscle or grace.

"I had to knock her out." The words come out in a cadence that matches his measured breathing.

The choppers are getting louder. Graham's heart is booming in his chest. To the east, a collection of black specks pepper the sky.

"Let me run, Graham," I say.

"Not yet." The tree line is about 300 yards away with zero cover. "Maybe when we're closer to the woods," he says, then adds, "I never hit a woman before."

"Don't think on it," I murmur.

"As soon as I let her go, she started turning dials and pressing buttons. Whatever she was doing, whoever she was calling, I had to stop her."

"You did right, Graham."

Graham

Mags is light in my arms, and the desperation fueling my veins makes my limbs pump like pistons.

I switch back and forth between sighting the steadily growing mechanical cloud of copters approaching from the east, and the trees transforming from a deep green-brown swipe of promise into trunks and limbs and leaves in front of us.

We gonna make it.

We gonna make it.

We gonna make it.

The explosion pops my body into the air. Mags flies outta my arms, and I'm eating dirt about ten yards from where she lands in a heap. "Mags!"

Though she's facedown, she's fanning her hands like she's making a snow angel in the dirt. When she lifts her head, she seems dazed. Then she winks, hops to her feet, and runs.

That's my Mags.

She's favoring her right foot, but she's zigzagging and making damn good time. I haul ass after her.

Another missile smashes the ground between us and a deluge of dirt rains down from the sky. We both stumble, but keep moving. I slow down some to let Mags keep ahead of me.

The next missile hits the middle of the first row of trees, right where we're headed. The copters sound like they're on top of us, but I don't got time to check the sky anymore. Mags veers west.

I stay right behind her.

Mags

When the missile hits the trees, rage consumes me. An icy cold wave of drenching sorrow follows. Same like when Ma's forest farm burned. My eyes burn and my left foot is numb. I'm gonna save the damned trees, and they're gonna save me.

I don't know how. I just believe with everything in me.

The shade welcomes me like a loving mother's arms.

Graham's pounding footsteps soften into thuds behind me.

I wanna sag and let my aching, depleted body fall down. Instead, I get as deep into the woods as I can. Yes, it's the woods.

A majestic tree, its trunk as thick as I am tall, obstructs me. I pull up short. The sound of the choppers is fading. Overhead, there's nothing but branches and leaves. Not one dot of sky. I stagger to the tree, throw my arms around it, and heave. It saps all my fear, all my pain, and fills the empty places left behind with relief and gratitude.

I'm alive.

I try not to think what would of happened to me if Graham hadn't showed up.

He stands real close behind me, covering my body with his, matching his arms to mine, and we hug the tree together. For the first time since Ma died, someone else's touch feels good.

I don't know how long we stand still and quiet, but by the time I let go, we don't hear the choppers anymore.

"They ain't chasing us." Awe fills my voice.

Graham pushes a glob of sweaty hair off my forehead. "Folks who put their faith in steel and concrete fear the wilderness." He gazes around us. "And these is some wild woods."

It's true. Now that my heart is resuming its normal beat, I hear insects and birds. It's like they're welcoming us and cheering us on.

"We're safe," Graham says.

I take hold of his hand and lead him south without another word.

seven

Mags

These woods is thicker and more mysterious than any I ever came across in the Free Territories, and living in em is making me stronger inside and out.

Every morning, I wake up feeling more true to my nature.

Despair silenced my voice when Ma died, but Graham coming to find me seems to have resurrected some innate ability to chatter about everything and nothing.

For about two weeks, I try to explain about why I left

him without one word. He keeps saying it's all right, but I cain't quit wanting to make him really understand.

Finally, one day, he sits me down on a fallen log. "Mags, I thought I knew how hard Ma's death hit you. And I thought I understood how it cut you a little deeper every day that Little Mother didn't come back to fetch you. But it wasn't until the day I woke up, and you were gone, that I really got how hard it's been for you, losing the people you love so deep."

My breath catches.

I don't bring the subject up again.

My chest and banged up foot is healing fast with the aid of Graham's salves and rubs. One day, when I'm marveling over his handiwork, I tell him, "You've got powerful healing hands."

He says: Just for you.

Those three words put a smile on my face that reaches deep, all the way down into the black hole. "I'm gonna call you Doc from now on."

He ruffles my hair, and says, "You call me whatever you want."

One night when I'm lying next to him, and he's got his arms wrapped around me, I tell him about Project Renew.

Up until now, I've wanted to push that abomination as far from my mind as possible. His body stiffens and his heart thumps as I relate the horror that Teddy gloated over.

"Well," he says, "knowing she gave birth to that monster eases my guilt over knocking his mother in the head."

"You still carrying that?" I ask.

"Not anymore."

"Good, cause we never would of got outta there if you hadn't done what you did."

We fall into a peaceful quiet, but I cain't quite fall asleep. We hain't come across a single other human or any settlements since we entered the woods. I got an itchy feeling we gonna, soon. "Doc, you still awake?" I whisper.

"Uh-huh."

"We gonna have to tell everyone we come across about Teddy, and what they done, and what they plan to do."

"Yep," he says.

Graham, he can be a man of few words. "Do you think people will take it to heart? It's kinda hard to believe if you hain't seen it with your own eyes."

"We cain't worry about whether or not they believe you. We just gotta sound the alarm."

Of course, he's right. It's just that talking to strangers ain't ever been my forte, as Ma would say.

Graham

Mags has always been the most beautiful girl I ever laid eyes on—so much so that no other girl has ever got my notice. But in the wilderness, Mags is subtly transforming. I swear her hair is growing thicker on her head, and her pale skin shimmers.

I don't waste my breath telling her not to worry. People

gonna think what they think when she tells em about Teddy. And I know it won't do a speck of good to calm her. She's just gonna have to experience it for herself. Anyone who sees Mags these days ain't ever gonna accuse her of lying.

She's got the presence of a saint born from the earth itself.

Mags

The man's and woman's faces are mud-stained, as are the faces of the three young children clinging to her filthy, torn skirt.

I raise my hand in peace.

The man holds out his arm, a bar in front of his wife.

Graham positions himself behind me, nonthreatening. I don't wanna blurt out the black warning I've gotta pass on without a few words of kindness first, if only to comfort myself. "You're the first people we seen in a long time," I say.

"If you want to see more people, keep heading south."

"Is that where you're from?" I ask.

"We aren't unioners," the man barks.

"Why not?" I ask the question without thinking. I cain't help it. I wanna hear his answer.

"The unioners are cowards. They aren't gonna fight the Kyintans. We're going to join the rebellion."

"The rebellion?"

"Up north, folks are banding together in the mountains. The Kyintans are weak. We can finally defeat them if we've got the courage."

Little Mother doesn't believe in war. War is nothing if not the will to dominate. The first tenet of the Gospel of Nature and Man is dominate nothing, not nature and not other people. Coexistence is the true path.

"Then you need to know what you might be facing on your journey," I say.

"What's that?"

"Project Renew."

The man and woman exchange glances. The smallest kid starts wailing. The woman picks him up to shush him.

The child quiets down but doesn't stop crying completely.

"Tell us what you've got to tell us, and be quick about it," the man gripes. "We've got a lot more ground to cover before night falls."

As I talk, the expressions on the man's and woman's faces shift from disinterest and curiosity, to anger and fear, respectively.

"Damn!" he explodes. "Why can't they just leave us alone to live the way we see fit? Why does some government always have to control us, like we haven't got minds of our own to think for ourselves?"

I'm relieved they don't doubt me.

"Which cities did they attack?" he asks.

"The only two I know for sure are Landis and Enniston, but there's eight others."

"Damn!" the man reiterates. "How will we know which road to take?"

"I don't know."

"Damn! Damn! Damn!"

The woman pulls the man aside. They whisper with one

another.

"Where are you from?" one of the children asks.

"The Free Territories," Graham answers.

"Where's that?"

"North and west of here."

The kid nods as if he understands, though I'm not sure he does.

The man and woman walk back toward Graham and me. "We're going to continue heading north," he says.

"But thank you for the warning," she adds.

Graham

The farther south we make our way, the more folks we come across that's heading north to join the rebellion. Everyone thanks Mags for her warning, but no one changes their mind about the direction they're headed, or their purpose.

We reach the first union community about two days after we shift our direction east. A small town of about 200 people, it makes me long for my Pa real bad, wishing he could see it. The few advancements that have been made in the Free Territories pale in comparison.

Everything about the small town is attuned to the natural world—the shops, what they eat, and what they wear. Even the way they treat one another—with a genuine respect—makes me understand that what has cost Mags a lot has benefited the world. Little Mother's Gospel ain't just a dream.

They welcome us with curiosity and open arms, even though Mags doesn't breathe a word about Little Mother being her mom.

The day after we arrive, when our bellies are full and we both got on a whole set of new clothes, a town meeting is called. Mags shares her sad news. Once she gets going, people hang on her every word. For all the years she hardly spoke, she has the gift of mesmerizing a crowd. Maybe more so than her mother. Shock and dismay ripple through the audience. This is the first any of em have heard about Project Renew. And though the news is bleak, they're grateful to Mags for bringing it to em.

The kinda folks drawn to the union vision is the kinda folks who love life and the earth that sustains it. The path they've chosen allows for more than mere belief, they're living it and experiencing the truth of it.

The Kyintan view of a flawed creation, which select men are called upon to improve, has been disproved by the breakdown and failure of Kyintan rule. Many of the folks in this town have lost loved ones to the urbanscapes, where flora and fauna were razed and populations degenerated physically, mentally, and emotionally on 100% synthetic diets. That the Kyintan remedy for their failures is to escalate their destruction of nature only outrages.

Later that night, the city's most skilled hackers program a massive schedule of news blurts over the internet. But within six seconds of the first transmission, their servers crash.

Over the next few days, an alternate plan is developed to disseminate the information. A letter is drafted. Volunteers will travel by horseback to five other union cities. Each city will be asked to send out five more volunteers to tag five more union cities. The towns on the borders and shores of the wilderness will be asked to bear the burden of spreading the alarm to the larger world, but the decision to do so will be at their discretion and according to their abilities and resources.

While the plans are being fine-tuned, Mags and I catch up with the news of the rest of the world.

The Corporation is crumbling hard and fast. Though the Kyintans maintain control over a percentage of land mass on every continent, pockets of rebellion are on the rise globally. Though there is no coordination, the rebellions share similar goals: overthrow Kyintan rule and arm the local populations.

Mags

I'll admit, it's awful and wonderful seeing what Little Mother's fanaticism has wrought. The citizens of the town are healthy and whole on every level. They're without disease, and their skin and eyes are clear. All of em stand straight, and keep busy with their work and the things that call to em. They grow their own food, like we done in the settlement when Ma was alive, and every meal we eat is more delicious than the last.

But the day I stumble upon a statue of Little Mother, a kinda shrine at the edge of the woods, I wanna punch it. Since I don't wanna break my fingers, I just kinda stalk around it with a cold gaze. Anger buried for years springs free.

Oh, I am gonna find my mom. And I am gonna let her have it.

Graham

Mags fumes for days after we come across the chapel in the woods. "They worship her like a damn god!"

"Folks need something tangible they can hold on to," I say.

"Did you see anyone holding onto that statue?"

"No, but—"

"Do you think she encourages that?"

"What?" I ask.

"Being worshipped?"

"How do I know?"

"What if it's all gone to her head and she's just like Teddy?"

"Now, Mags, Little Mother stands for the opposite of everything Teddy has ever done."

"Not if she encourages folks to view her like a god."

I cain't well argue her point. "Don't make up your mind about anything until you talk to her."

"Maybe I don't wanna talk with her anymore. Maybe we'll just stay right here and never leave."

"I don't think you're gonna have peace until you see her again."

"I can see her anytime I want on the internet."

"You need to see her face to face."

"Why? Does she even know Ma died? Does she even care?"

"I don't know, Mags. I just don't know. She's the only one who can answer your questions." I don't remind her she's the one who told me that not so long ago.

"To tell the truth, Graham, right now, I don't even care to give her the time a day. She might be my mother by blood, but I hain't seen her for—" She calculates on her fingers. "—almost ten years. She never came back to the settlement to see how Ma or me was doing. She never even sent me a letter, and you know other people in the settlement got mail. If she'd sent me something, I would of got it. No, I got my mother figured out. She's one of those kinda people who cares about ideas more than anything else. And now she's famous, what does she need a pissed off daughter around for?"

"She probly doesn't know you're mad."

Mags presses her back against a big ole tree and narrows her eyes. "Oh, I bet she knows I'm mad. I bet that's why I hain't heard nothing from her. If the unioners knew what kinda mother she really was, don't you think it might taint her reputation? Maybe then folks wouldn't be so all fired up to bow down and pray to her, like she's something better than the rest of us."

"It's all a lot of speculation until you talk with her direct."

Mags cocks her knee and slams the sole of her boot against the poor, innocent tree. Then she stalks off before I can get in another word.

I hope Little Mother is ready for the reunion with her daughter. It's gonna be some fireworks.

Mags

I'm finally ready to head out to Union Major. Though I'm still not sure how I feel about Little Mother. We've got a ways to go, maybe 1500 miles, before I got to decide. We ask around the town about how much a good horse would cost. We don't have any money, but we have some skills. I'm good with growing anything you can plant in the ground, and Doc's good with healing anything that hurts.

Karl, one of the town bigwigs, invites us to his home. He's got a large family, and they make us feel right welcome. After we're done eating dinner, Karl and his youngest boy take us out back and lead us to a pasture.

The boy whistles, and the most beautiful horse in the world comes running. It's black and white, and it manages to steal my heart in some new way.

Karl waves his hand, and the horse stops short of where we're standing.

I can see the gleam in its dark eyes and the luster of sweat on its withers.

Karl goes over and nuzzles the horse's neck. "We want to help you reach Union Major before the first snowfall," he says. "Which, by the way, seems to come earlier every year. Cochise is young and curious; she has the endurance to make the trip."

My heart is beating up and down and sideways. I want this horse. But me and Graham are gonna have to work the whole winter before we can pay for her. "How much does a horse like that cost?"

"We mean to give her to you."

"I cain't accept such a gift." Can I?

"Please. It's a gift, from the whole town, for the Prophet."

I'm confused.

Karl's son's eyes are bright when they meet mine. "That's what they're calling you on the internet."

"The Kyintans could have kept Project Renew quiet much longer, and killed a lot more innocents if you'd not sounded the alarm," Karl says. "The whole union is grateful to you."

I don't know what to say, but tears are stinging my eyes. "Cochise," I whisper. Then, "Thank you." It's all I can muster before a tidal wave of gratitude swells up in me and washes my poor battered heart out to sea. I turn around so they won't have to watch me blubber like a big baby.

Karl's son spends the next week training me and Cochise to ride together, and training her to separate from the herd. Once I'm comfortable, Graham joins us. I'm a little bit miffed when my horse seems to take to Doc quicker than she did to me, but I guess I'll live, since I love them both so much.

After a long day of riding, we settle down for the night.

I've already dozed off when a loud pop wakes me. It's hard to orient myself with Cochise squealing. My legs are curled up to my chest, but Graham's warmth ain't against my back. It was when I drifted off. I get up on my knees and stretch out my arms in every direction. "Graham," I whisper. "Graham."

"Mags." When my eyes adjust, I see his tall shadow next to Cochise.

I crawl then run, trying to get as close to them as possible. Cower behind Graham is more like it. He's trying to calm Cochise down, but every few minutes there's another pop.

The shouts and wails of the dying fill our ears. We're hearing gun shots.

I stop counting at twenty.

Graham manages to quiet Cochise's cries, but her hooves ain't even close to still. She's stamping the ground and making a ruckus.

Finally, the gunfire stops. So do the screams. For a few minutes, the woods is total quiet.

Then we hear the voices talking in a foreign language. They're headed straight for us.

I want to bolt, but we'd be running blind.

The voices grow louder. By the time they drown out the sound of my blood drumming in my ears, we can see the lights dancing, sweeping through the woods. They're searching for us.

I try to keep count of the voices. We're outnumbered by at least three or four.

Graham's head is bowed, with one hand buried in Cochise's mane, and the other squeezing my hand.

I force myself to stand as still as I've ever stood in my entire life. Cochise freezes, too, as if she understands the choice before us: Be quiet or die. But I cain't die like this. Not after everything I've been through. I need more days with Graham. A lot more. I gotta ride Cochise again and again.

The dark hides most of us, but the white dapples in Cochise's coat glow in the night. When the lights transform from spotlights to sweeping arcs, I cain't stay still any longer. "Graham, we gotta run."

He squeezes my hand so tight it hurts. I search his face, trying to read what he's thinking. His head is cocked to one side, listening. I pause long enough to listen with him.

The faint thwack of a chopper sounds overhead.

Cochise strains at the rope still knotted around the tree.

Graham lets go of my hand and grips my shoulder hard. "Hold still," he says.

"What if they're bringing more men with more guns?"

Cochise squeals so loud that for a few seconds I'm deaf. Every single light swings in our direction. I attack the knot in Cochise's rope with trembling fingers. It don't budge.

As the chopper gets louder, I crouch down for the knife I hide in my boot.

The tree leaves and bushes are shaking from the wind of the chopper's blades.

More shouting. The lights that have been searching for

us flash up, disappearing into the halo of light where the chopper hovers.

My ears strain for clues about what's coming.

Except for the fingers he brushes across the top of my head, Graham remains still as a statue. Usually, his calm nature soothes me, but I'm so wound up I just want to kick him into gear. Why are we just standing here?

The voices are climbing, fading into the sound of the chopper's loud engine. They're leaving, not sending reinforcements.

I'm not sure how long we stand there. Once silence envelops us, we collapse, but don't sleep.

Cochise remains skittish the next morning.

"Wait here," Graham says.

"Be careful," I tell him. Some part of me knows he's gonna find something terrible, and I don't even want him to go look. But I know I cain't stop him. If someone survived, he'll want to nurse them back to health. I'm proud of him, but so scared of what he's gonna find.

I focus on the tangles in Cochise's mane, aiming to keep my fingers as light as possible. The task soothes her. But the longer we wait, the heavier my heart gets.

When I cain't stand being separated from Graham one minute longer, I try to lead Cochise in the direction he went. But the stubborn horse won't go. I tug on her rope and she flattens her ears and snorts. When I yank harder on her rope, she rolls her eyes and rears up. Stubborn thing. I'm only half-angry.

There's a patch of sunlight in the opposite direction, so I lead her toward that. She's docile. After a little while she lies down to sun. I pace the glade until I admit I'm spent too and rest against her back with my eyes closed.

The sound of rattling brush stirs me. Graham is calling. I rush toward him.

His white face, and the mud and dark brown streaks on his shirt and pant leg, confirm my worst fears. When he breaks down in my arms, we both stagger backward.

"Forty-three," he says.

I don't know what he means.

"Forty-three." He says it over and over.

I finally get his meaning. I cain't think of anything to say, so I just hold him tighter.

When he pulls away from me, I grab his hand. He doesn't look me in the eye when he tells me what he saw.

"Forty-three young men shot execution style with bags over their heads and their hands tied behind their backs. Every one of them was shot in the back. I started to bury them." He holds his hands up. They're black with mud. "There were too many. I just gave up. But I covered em. With leaves and branches." He breaks down again.

Graham has always been strong for me. This time I gotta be strong for him.

We don't say much the rest of the day.

Ma used to say that folks take drugs cause their brains are in pain. Maybe she was right and maybe she was wrong, but stumbling upon a cartel's brutal remains is a bitter reminder of how far humanity has to go.

Graham and I don't talk about what would have happened if that chopper hadn't come when it did. It doesn't seem right, counting our blessings when so many others have died.

eight

Mags

It takes us about a month of traveling east before we reach Union Major. The first and largest union community, it's Little Mother's home base. With a population in the thousands, the city ain't quick nor easy to get around.

I make it clear to Graham I'm gonna talk to Little Mother, but it's gonna be in my own time. Since I don't know exactly when that might be, I cain't tell him more than that. He doesn't press or bother me none on the subject, which I appreciate.

Graham and I've been doing work in the towns we stopped at along the way. After I made sure news about Project Renew had reached a city, Graham and I would trade our services for room, board for ourselves and Cochise, and supplies. He'd do some healing, and I'd help with the gardens or on the farms. Some of the folks paid us with the new union coins.

By the time we reach Union Major, we have a sock full. We ain't rich, but we have enough to rent a nice suite of rooms next to a lazy river, and a stall for Cochise around the corner.

The sound of rushing water has always soothed me, and I need to be soothed. Statues and likenesses of Little Mother are all over the damned city. One afternoon, when I'm at the market and Graham is tending to a sick little one, I draw a mustache on one of the statues. It is a right dumb thing to do, but it makes me feel a little better.

The next day Graham points out a picture of the defaced statue on the internet. I cain't hide my smirk. I know he knows I did it, but he doesn't chide me. None of the comments on the post is positive. Some folks even go as far to suspect a traitor and nonbeliever has infiltrated their sacred refuge.

"Makes their preaching about coexistence a bit superficial, don't it?"

Graham just gives me a hug and takes me by the hand. We loop around to pick up Cochise before he leads me down to the river. Once the horse is grazing, we settle near by. Graham stares at the grass as he tells me what he obviously needs to unburden.

Graham

"I saw Little Mother the other day," I say. When Mags doesn't say a word, I raise my head.

"Well?" She doesn't meet my gaze. "Tell me all about it." Her voice is brittle.

"There's not so much to tell. She was in the middle of a crowd—"

Mags snorts. "Was the queen wearing her golden crown?"

"Maybe it's time to let her know we're here. Maybe it's time to have it out with her, so you can get on with your life."

"And you can get on with yours?"

"I'm on with my life. My life is you."

"Easy for you to say," she mutters before getting to her feet and pacing with her arms locked across her chest.

I wait, knowing she ain't near done releasing the turmoil inside.

"What am I gonna do? Go up and give her a big hug?"

"If giving her a hug feels false, then don't do it."

"What if she refuses to see me?"

"Why would she do that?"

Mags shrugs. "I don't know, but I'm...I don't know, Graham. Maybe I'm just scared."

"It's all right to be scared, Mags."

"Of your own mother? That don't seem right to me."

"I think you've got her built up so big in your mind that the only way she's gonna become right-sized again is to get this over with. We stopped at plenty of towns along

148

the way that would of been a great place to build a life, but we didn't stay. You need to see Little Mother. It's why you came all this way."

Mags flops down next to me, spins on her butt, and lets her head drop into my lap. Progress. "I got you, Doc. And Cochise. If Little Mother don't want me, I'm gonna be all right."

"Yes, you will, Mags. Yes, you will."

Mags

Graham offers to come with me, but I wanna do this alone.

Little Mother lives in a small house in the center of town. It doesn't stand out or look special in any way. At first, I think I've read the address wrong, but I check it three times.

I walk back and forth in front of the house more than once. But then I get my nerve up and knock on the front door.

A woman answers the door. She looks too much like Ma looked when she was young. "May I help you?"

She don't even recognize me. A sharp, invisible knife twists in my chest. "I heard you don't mind folks stopping by to discuss the gospel."

"That's true." She motions me inside. "I always welcome a sincere discussion, and relish the chance to sharpen my wits." She leads me down a hall and out onto a patio. It's a wooden deck, built around an enormous magnolia tree.

With no permission from me, my eyes start to water. "Pretty tree," I say.

She nods.

"Does it have special meaning to you?"

She gets this faraway look in her eyes, and my heart gallops with hope. For her to recognize me—as her own flesh and blood, right this instant—is the line she's gotta cross if I'm gonna forgive her. "Yes, yes it does." She comes back to the present. "Can I get you something to drink?"

Maybe I'll give her a few more minutes to figure it out. "Sure, whatever you're having." My voice is kinda quavery, but she doesn't seem to notice.

"I'll be right back."

She returns with two glasses and a jug of ice water on a tray. She tells me to sit, fills a glass, and hands it to me before she takes a seat across from me.

My patience has evaporated like the short lead on a stick of dynamite. "You don't even recognize me, do you?"

A shadow falls across her face and her brows quirk. Then her lips spasm and her hands fly to the sides of her face. "Magnolia Bud?" She's outta her chair and bending over me, pulling me to her.

I'm stiff as a board in her arms. She failed. I'm convinced, without my prompting, I would of left her home still a stranger.

But she's weeping and laughing. It takes her some time to register I'm not responding in kind. Not even close. She pulls back, reaches for a napkin, and dabs at her eyes. "How's Ma?" she asks. "I'm surprised she didn't come with you."

"She couldn't. She's dead."

Little Mother covers her face with her hands. She returns to her seat and steadies herself by clinging to the side of the chair. Maybe if she didn't hold onto something she'd crumple to the floor. I think that's good. I'm hoping the news has made whatever black hole exists inside her real big.

When she sits back down, her face is bleached of all color. I note the tremble to her hands that wasn't there before I told her about Ma. "When?" The small question is quiet. Her voice ain't ringing out like it does on the videos. "What happened?"

I shrug. "The Corporation, drug cartels. We was never sure who started the fire."

"Fire?"

"They set the forest farm on fire. She burned with her trees. It's been almost five years now."

Her hands shake even worse. "I didn't know."

"No? I guess you never troubled yourself to find out. Posing for all those statues probly takes a lot of time."

She presses her hands against her thighs to still their shaking. "Those statues...I can't stop them. I've tried."

"Sure you did."

"You're hurt deeply," she says. "I can see that. I expect I'd be hurt, too, if I were you."

"Except you ain't me," I say. "Ma didn't ever leave you and never come back."

She works her jaw. "I'm glad you're here, Mags. I'm glad you came to see me."

"I bet you are. It sure would of been nice if you'd ever bothered to come and see me."

"If I could have, I would have. There's a bounty on my head. It's not safe for me to leave the wilderness."

I shake my head. In real life, she's a right disappointment. "You don't need to tell me nothing about not being safe."

She extends her hands.

I ignore the offer. "Things changed a lot in the settlement when Ma died."

"How so?"

It's a cautious question, like maybe she don't really wanna know. "You remember Franny?"

"I do."

"She and Da run the settlement now. They're passing all kinds of laws. They passed a law that every girl and boy gotta get married and start breeding on their 15th birthday. The MBO—marriage and breeding ordinance, it's called—is what spurred me to leave. It's what made me cross a goddamned continent to find you."

She worries with her hands in her lap.

"But don't fear none. Da's not near as popular as you. They hadn't made any statues of him by the time I left."

"That's not fair, Mags."

"Oh, Little Mother, don't you be talking about what's fair with me," I growl.

"You're right. But you being hateful and angry toward me won't change the fact that it's so good to see you! I'm so proud that you made it all this way. What a journey. Did you make the trip alone?"

"Part way. Till Graham caught up with me and saved my

damned life," I mutter. I don't bother to tell her about Cochise. I doubt she could understand how much the horse means to me.

"Graham? Is he the same boy who stuck to you like glue from the moment he could toddle?"

"Yep."

Something about her remembering Graham and me when we was little scrapes the raw inside me.

"You said he saved your life."

"Yep. That scientist who created the pathogen for Project Renew was gonna use my healthy ovaries for research. If Graham didn't showed up when he did, I'd be Test Subject 122K right about now."

Little Mother clutches at a small gold locket on a chain around her neck. It's exactly like the one Ma wore with the picture of her beloved in it. Little Mother stands and points at me. "You're the Prophet."

I roll my eyes. Based on my reports and union activism, Project Renew ain't highly classified no more. The entire world knows what Teddy was up to. He's in hiding, and the rebellion has made impressive inroads in dismantling what's left of the Corporation.

Little Mother crosses her arms and rubs em up and down as she walks back and forth in front of me. "My little Magnolia Bud is the Prophet." She shakes her head. "I should have known." She stands still. "You were so tiny and so fierce from the moment you were born. There was something so strong and sturdy about you. It's why I named you Magnolia. Magnolia trees are strong, ancient, and beautiful." She reaches out and plays with the ends of my hair.

When I jerk my head, she drops her hand.

"I'd never have left you, if...if..." She pauses. "Mags, you never needed me, not from the moment you were born."

"Is that the bullshit you tell yourself to help you sleep at night? I was five years old when you left! Of course I needed you!"

"But I didn't leave you alone. You had Ma."

"I was eleven years old when Ma died. I tried to save

her. But I was too small. I went crazy with grief and guilt. If it hadn't been for Graham, I would of."

"Mags, if I'd known—"

"Yeah, it's becoming real clear to me that if you'd known, you would of done nothing! Little Mother's a right fit name for you." I hold my thumb and index finger barely apart from one another. "Cause you just about this much of a mother."

She closes her eyes in defeat. We both know I'm right. It's clear she wasn't ever up to the job of caring for a child.

"Do all those people who think you fell outta heaven even know you have a daughter?"

"No, they don't."

"I didn't think so." I feel a smidge better that she stops defending herself, but I'm not done making my point. "So people just drop by here, all the time, and you sit around on this deck, talking about doctrine and principles and stuff?" I don't know why that thought gets me so riled up, but it does. My heart's racing around my chest, sending energetic pulses down my legs and out my arms. "But you never had a moment to sit down and write me a letter? Not once in over ten years?"

"Mags, if I'd had any idea how much it would have meant to you, I would have written."

I push myself up from the sofa and stalk across the deck. When I reach the door that leads into the house, I turn to say one more thing. "How could you not know I would of given anything to hear from my own mother? How could you not have known? There's videos of you plastered all over the internet, sermoning and preaching, and pouring all of yourself into strangers. But not a single word or minute for me. I'm your daughter, and you live like I don't even exist!"

I march toward the front door. I reckon I said what I came to say.

She runs after me.

When her hand touches my shoulder, I whirl around. "Don't touch me. You don't got the right."

She recoils, like I'm a snake spitting venom. "I don't blame you for being angry with me, Mags. Not at all. But I never forgot you. Don't ever tell yourself I did. Every day, I—"

"And don't you ever think for a minute that it's gonna be all right between you and me. Cause it never is!" My blood is boiling hot. I can barely think straight. "I'm the one who walked almost 3000 miles to find you. But from the day you left the settlement, you didn't raise a goddamn twig to see me."

Graham

"I'm glad you talked to her," I say.

"It didn't do no good," Mags says.

"Yeah, it did."

"Then why do I feel so bad?"

"Mags, you got so many emotions about Little Mother, and they's layered and buried deep over so many years, I reckon it's gonna take a little time to let it all out."

"She looks so much like Ma. That's what hurts the most. I miss Ma. I hate how she died. That she burned alive." Finally, Mags breaks down in front of me.

I hold her until she's spent. "Feel better?" I ask after she's quiet and still awhile.

"Maybe a little bit."

Over the next few weeks, Mags and I fall back into the routine we been in since we arrived in Union Major. Mags working at one of the big nurseries, and me helping out at a clinic, treating the immigrants who pour into the city every day. In the evenings, we walk Cochise out to the open space along the river. I usually sit under a tree while Mags runs her horse until they're both spent. It does all three of us good. Cochise has gotten friendly with the horse that stables next to her, and me and Mags sleep soundly most nights. Every now and then, I wake up in a cold sweat, with the image of 43 young dead men plastered to my eyelids.

An authorized missive comes for Mags at the end of summer.

The northern rebellion has Teddy in custody and they're gonna put him on trial. They need to confirm whether the popular rumors is true. Did Teddy confess his crimes directly to her?

Once she confirms he did, the official summons follows. They want her to testify at the trial. The lawyers and film crew will come to Union Major, and her testimony, along with the rest of the proceedings, will be broadcast live all over the world. The global event will serve as a different kinda Project Renew.

Kyintan world rule has ended and its philosophy about dominating nature has fallen outta popularity.

nine

Mags

Me and Graham take the day of my 16th birthday off from work. We sleep in late, with plans to take Cochise and follow the river into the woods later in the day. It's something we like to do whenever we get the chance. The woods in the wilderness is so powerful.

I stir first when the knock comes at the door. I bump Graham's shoulder. "You expecting company?"

"No."

I'm already wide awake, so I stop him from getting

outta bed. "I'll get it."

After slipping into my favorite baggy pants and T-shirt, I peek out the window. Little Mother's standing on our doorstep. I press my hands against my mouth. What's she doing here? My heart bucks like something wild. Does she remember today is my birthday? Does it matter to me if she does? Since our first ugly exchange, we've left each other alone.

Sometimes a longing to make peace with her tugs at me, but it's always fleeting and easy to ignore.

She knocks again.

I perform a nervous little jig in a circle. Will it kill me to open the door? Curiosity gets the upper hand on my forever-simmering anger.

"Magnolia, happy birthday!"

She shoves a scroll into my hand before I can protest. Being as trees are revered by most unioners, old-style books with paper made from cellulose ain't too popular anywhere in the wilderness. A popular method of making paper has been refined using a mix of dried leaves, grass, and rags. The texture is real durable, and scrolls are most often used whenever a hard copy of something is required or desired.

The scroll has ceramic handles. They look like they've been hand painted. It kinda touches me that she's come to give me a present. "Thank you."

"When you get a chance, maybe you can read it," she says.

"Okay." The fight has drained right outta me. I'm not right sure where it's gone, but its exit has left me feeling soft and not wanting her to leave right away. "What's it about?"

"It's a fairy tale, written a long time ago by a man named Hans Christian Andersen. It's called The Dryad. Dryads are tree spirits."

Something zings inside me when she says that. "You wanna come in for a minute?"

"I'd love to."

Graham is already preparing tea. "You two go on ahead and get comfortable. I'll have this ready in a minute."

We sit down in a couple of chairs in the front room.

"So you gonna testify at the trial?" Ma asks.

My jaw clenches. My name and face seem to be on some internet feed every single day. "Is that why you're here? Now that I'm famous like you, you finally interested in me?"

"The only reason I'm here is to wish my daughter happy birthday." She sounds kinda convincing.

"Why'd you bring me this story?"

"Ma gave me a copy of the book on my 16th birthday, right before I was pregnant with you."

"So now you kinda passing it on to me?"

"If you have any questions after you read it, please don't hesitate to come by the house."

"Did you have questions for Ma after you read it?"

"I did."

"Did she give you answers?" I ask.

"Yes."

"Ma had a locket, the same as the one you got on. Whose picture do you carry in yours?"

She opens it, stands up, and comes toward me. When she leans over, I recognize the picture of my newborn self. My name, Magnolia Bud, and my birthdate are engraved on the right side of the locket.

God, I hate when my eyes start watering and my heart starts melting all at once. "You wear that all the time?"

She crouches down in front of me and rests her hands on my knees. "I do."

"So you didn't forget about me?" I'm a blubbering lost cause and do nothing to fight the fingers she runs through my hair.

"Never. I always carried you in my heart. I always will."

I know it's true. It's why I always felt close to her, even when she was far away. It's why I knew she loved me, even when she never came back to get me.

"Your Ma, me, and now you," she says, "we've got gifts. Things we need to give the world. I had a calling, and it overpowered me. It's taken me to a lot of dangerous places, places I couldn't take a little girl, no matter how fearless and strong she is."

"Okay, then," I said. "I'll read the story."

Graham

Mags and Little Mother don't hear me enter the room, so I stand real still with the tray of tea and eggs mixed with greens and butter in my hand.

In that moment, it's clear to me that everything is gonna be all right with Mags. For the first time since she was five years old, she's whole.

When Little Mother rises, I finally cough and speak. "Anybody hungry?"

"I could eat a pound of bacon," Mags says.

"Sorry, don't got none," I say.

She starts laughing and doesn't stop. It's the sound of joy giving birth.

Mags

"Are we dryads?" I ask Little Mother. I have the scroll with me. "Is that the meaning of you giving me this story?" I've given it a lot of thought, and me and Graham have stayed up late many nights talking about its meaning.

"It would be hard to believe if it were true, wouldn't it?" Little Mother asks.

"Yep, it sure would."

"And yet, Ma died with her trees. I've spent my life preaching about the sacredness of nature, and you gotta green thumb that could revive a dead world."

"But I wasn't able to revive Ma's tree farm." That failure still dogs me.

"You understand, now, why that's just about the only thing you couldn't grow, don't you?"

"No, Little Mother. I don't. I poured all of myself into those seedlings for three long years, and about all I managed was some pathetic shoots that wilted and yellowed, no matter how much water or sunlight or mulch I nursed em with."

"When Ma was gone, those trees left with her."

Her words fall like dominoes as I trace a long row of memory.

"Her spirit and the life of those trees were interconnected," Little Mother says.

Graham

The next year, when the trial starts, Little Mother and Mags grow tight. Little Mother helps Mags handle the stark glare of the world spotlight, and stands by her side, right through all the stress and pressures of filming and being questioned by Teddy's lawyers.

When it's over, and Teddy is convicted, Mags asks me if it's all right if we stay and make our life in Union Major. I tell her I've gotten real used to the city and it would be hard for me to leave now.

"Then maybe we need to send for your Pa."

I say, "Maybe we do."

Today's not the day to tell her he ain't gonna come. He ain't gonna leave my mother, buried in the Free Territories.

I don't doubt that Ma, Little Mother, and Mags are dryads.

How can I? To look at em, with their dark hair (before it grayed on Ma and started turning gray on Little Mother), long, pale limbs, and leaf-shining eyes, is to witness a tree come to life.

"I reckon that makes me a tree shepherd or something," I say to Mags one day when we walk through the woods.

"Or something." She grins.

After the trial and its circus is over, and folks are sick and tired of hearing every sound bite, the world settles down. Little Mother can travel outside the borders of the wilderness and preach anywhere now.

The numbers of unioners are growing. So are the members of the rebellion, though there ain't really nothing left to rebel against.

The world lies in a peaceful stretch.

Mags

"You just gonna wreck the whole house?" I cain't believe

it. "Just for the sake of that tree?"

"That's your tree, Mags. I planted it the year the house was built, on your eleventh birthday."

I suck in my breath. "The year Ma died."

"I know. And like her forest farm was connected to her, this tree is connected to you. It needs to grow as big as it can. By this time next year, it's gonna be straining against the boards in the deck."

"Then just rip out the deck, but leave the rest of your house be."

"Have you noticed that this home is in the center of Union Major?"

I hain't really thought about it.

"But your magnolia tree is dead center. It's time to take all the statues of me down. My days as a figurehead are done. I need to fade. The only thing I want unioners to ever think about and remember is the sacred union of life and nature. Your magnolia tree, growing to its full height and reach, in the center of Union Major, the first and largest union city, is going to be the eternal symbol that burns in their hearts."

"Sounds like pretty ambitious aspirations for a tree."

"You'll see," Little Mother says. "You'll see."

Graham

As time goes on, Little Mother goes out to preach less and less, until she doesn't go at all. By the time she enters seclusion, unioners from all over the world are making pilgrimages to Mags' tree. Over the years, it's gotten to be over 65 feet high with a circumference of shade over 150 feet around.

The day Cochise lies down beneath that tree to never get back up, we all old. Me and Mags are well past 50, and Little Mother's 70th birthday is long come and gone. I'm worried how Mags is gonna handle her dear horse's passing, but she takes it pretty well.

"Do you remember that night in the wilderness, Graham? The night we thought we was gonna die?"

"I hain't ever forgot it."

"Me either," she whispers.

"I hain't forgot the folks who died."

"Me either."

Although we've never talked about that night, she's familiar with the night sweats that still pull me from my sleep.

"That night all I could think was: I gotta have more days with Graham. I gotta ride Cochise again. That was my prayer and it's been answered many times over. I got a lot to be thankful for," she says. "Those boys you found didn't get a chance to take another breath."

"I know, Mags. I know."

"Cochise died a peaceful death with the folks who loved her by her side."

Tears are rolling down my face.

"I won't ever forget those boys who died—" She gulps. "Like Ma, for no good reason at all."

I put my arm around her and we sit quiet for a long time. Death may be part and parcel of life, but the meaningless death of those we love will always feel like being damned.

The Tree Hugger

When Little Mother passes, Mags tells me it doesn't hurt near as much as it did when Ma died.

"For one thing, she lived her full days. The other was she died without pain. It's how I wanna go," she says. "Close to my tree."

I don't remind her that Little Mother didn't have a tree.

"All trees is her," she says, as if she's read my mind. "But instead of dying with her when she passed, they just let her go."

Who am I to argue?

Mags gives me a pair of woven chairs on my hundredth birthday. We set em out beneath her tree, so we can greet as many folks who come to visit as possible.

I'm not sure how or when I died, but now I linger on the edge of two worlds, waiting for Mags to join me for our next big adventure.

ten

Mags

The lights are hot and the reflective panels intensify their warmth. They've caked my face with makeup and it feels like it's dripping down my neck. But I don't move to wipe the trickles away. The only thing that will achieve is a goopy hand, which an intern will have to wipe off as if I were a two-year-old.

Experience always serves. That's one of my sayings, not Ma's and not Little Mother's. A twinge of pride tickles my heart. As much as I loved those two, and as much as they influenced who I've become, I'm satisfied that my personal understandings have blossomed beyond what they both taught me.

I'm seated in my woven chair; the matching one beside me is empty. It was Doc's. A young man drags a director's chair to my other side. Sydney Graville will sit in it soon. He's wanted to interview me on a live screen feed for over a decade. He's not exactly a believer in the union, but he loves a good story, and in my old age, I've become a good story.

Now that the Corporation has long since been abolished, and union researchers are making breathtaking contributions to the advancement of mankind, more and more people are curious about how we live: in harmony with nature, never dominating anyone or anything.

Ma passed on a way of living to Little Mother and to me. Little Mother made believers out of millions, but Graham and I became celebrated heroes for breaking the news about Project Renew and testifying against Teddy.

The Tree Hugger

Graham passed last year, and every day he's gone, I lose more strength and have less of a will to live. It won't be long before the Earth reclaims me too. That's why I agreed to do this one last interview with Sydney.

Two nights later, I awake to a strong sense of Graham's presence. I leave my small home barefoot, and lie down next to his grave, beneath my tree.

I don't close my eyes, because I want to see this big old world one more time.

When Graham's spirit hovers above me, I say goodbye to my body that has been such a good home to me for so many long years. I forget all the pain of my journey as sensations of pleasure course through me.

It's the joy, not the sorrow that counts.

When the last bit of attachment to my body has drained away, Graham's spirit beckons. To say we fly hand in hand would be a poor explanation of what's happening. It's more like we have no skin between us, and no obstacles around us, like every emotion is pure and energetic, propelling us, and our love for one another, to a destination that yearns for our arrival.

The tree shepherd guides his beloved dryad to her eternal home, deep in the heart of the cosmic forest.

Author's Note

The Tree Hugger, a Dystopian Fairy Tale is a retelling of Hans Christian Andersen's "The Dryad". I absolutely love the idea of spirits whose lives are connected to trees. However, in the original tale, the dryad is flighty (really?) and curious. As is often the case in fairy tales, that curiosity doesn't go unpunished.

I had to ask: What is wrong with wanting to see more of the world?

Nothing!

So, on those two counts, I altered the tale. Rather than the flighty creature in Andersen's tale, I believe a nature-spirt born with a direct relationship to trees would be steady, solid, focused, and determined. Thus, Mags was born. More apt to be silent and solitary, sturdy and resilient than whimsical and capricious.

And what about that trip? The fact that Andersen's dryad got punished for her curiosity and sense of adventure didn't sit well with me. I wanted my tree hugger to find joy at the end of her journey, to rise above her trials and tribulations.

Mags is also curious when she leaves home. But her

curiosity is driven from a deep wound. And though her journey isn't characterized by whimsy, there are some wild woods and a bit of enchantment along the way.

Thank You

I appreciate you spending your valuable time reading *The Tree Hugger*. If you'd like to share the story with other readers, please tell a friend, or post a review on any book-ish site.

I'd also like to invite you to sign up for my newsletter: http://eepurl.com/wWKUj. It's quirky—like me:D—and I confess, it comes out sporadically, but I send a variety of things, including some (hopefully) pleasant surprises along with updates on all my new releases.

Sincerely,

First Chapter

of

I Am Lily Dane

No, Lily. Not the butterflies!

Her belly curdles. The sour aftertaste ascends, surging in the back of her throat. She glances from side to side. No one is watching her: the cause of her bitter emotions. Around us, everyone is fascinated by the speckled wings of brilliant colors fluttering, flitting, flying among the zinnias and lilacs.

Only I am privy to Lily's desire to crush and dismember.

Frantic, I intensify my rebuke. *Lily Dane! They're helpless!*

She darts forward.

Helpless...

The girl never heeds my pleas. My only consolation is her target's escape. To the insect's warning system, her clumsy abruptness blares like a siren. Unfortunately, my Lily is nothing if not determined.

She registers her failure as tactical information and regroups.

The capture of a butterfly requires stealth, and perhaps numbers to increase the odds of success.

I groan as she edges away from her parents and winds along a little-traveled dirt trail. After several turns, she smiles.

Except for seven sapphire-winged butterflies sipping from a puddle of mud, this isolated section of the butterfly habitat is empty.

Lily's tiny, controlled steps are imperceptible. Her hand swipes in the blink of an eye. Six creatures scatter.

With her fist deep in the pocket of her Juicy Couture velour hoody, Lily crushes the poor insect with nimble fingers.

When Spencer and Blair Dane find her, their nine-year-old daughter's face beams.

When I found myself bound to Lily Dane in the cosmic ethers where shadows and souls unite, I cried out for a liberty that could never be granted. My repulsion—born from the most elemental substances comprising our forms—persisted throughout our shared life, in the womb and beyond.

Lily was a monster from the moment of conception. Not a blood-sucking, razor-toothed, gut-you-with-her-claws monster. No, she was a glacial, psychological predator.

Imagine yourself naked and defenseless in the dead of winter's brutal snow, without garments or heat, and how the pervasive chill numbs and paralyzes before it kills you without a word. Then imagine this scene infinite; your existence upon the frigid spiritual tundra extends days, weeks, years, with no relief on the horizon. Death's embrace begins to appeal, a mirage of warmth.

It makes sense—the obsession that ending Lily's life

would become for me. Impotence only fueled my preoccupation. But I'm getting ahead of myself. Allow me to start from the beginning, with Lily's parents.

Spencer and Blair Dane were united in unholy matrimony for the sole purpose of accelerating their social ascension. A hedge fund manager, Spencer appreciated his wife's degree in art history. She appeared cultivated, while offering zero risk of professional competition. Theirs was a marriage of clarity; neither love nor affection complicated the emotional wasteland of their union.

However, after a particularly icy patch, Blair had occasion to view the film *The War of the Roses*. It was a random act—she considered all commercial entertainment lowbrow—which she indulged in on a whim after a few too many glasses of Pinot Noir, while Spencer was away on a business trip. The undignified spectacle of the dissolution of the Rose marriage seized Blair's imagination with a premonitory grip. The following morning in yoga class, she continued to dwell on the movie's most disturbing scenes. The message became more personalized.

The universe (she went to Wellesley and didn't believe in God or god) (please!) had provided her with a clear and potent glimpse of the future were she to divorce her charming, conceited, and manipulative husband.

The message: There could be no recovery from such an act for Blair Dane.

However, this insight did nothing to repair the Grand Canyon-sized gash in the Dane marriage.

She studied the tabloids for solutions. The images of taut, glowing mothers contradicted Blair's view of childbearing as the most direct route to mar her perfect, if frosty, figure. Stars were bouncing back after giving birth. Many looked even better than before.

If nothing else, Blair was strategic. Photoshop was considered as a cofactor in the matrix of her calculations. She couldn't expect to look as perfect as the glossy pictures, but better a few stretch marks than death by chandelier.

Spencer was intrigued.

Blair could almost hear the gears in his brain whir when she proposed the superglue that would hold their arctic union together.

A child.

Her husband favored all things that gave him an edge. Blair would artfully arrange the deal-enhancing, family photo spreads on his massive mahogany desk herself.

When she became pregnant with a girl, they agreed on the name Lily. Blair interpreted this minor accord as another direct message from the universe: Your daughter, Lily Dane, will be your savior.

This is where I entered the picture, condemned by fate to be the deified Lily's shadow for the duration of my existence.

Being a shadow is not a bad thing per se. Although considered dark, we travel light. Among other things, we serve as a reservoir for non-matter imbalances, which can't be rectified instantaneously in time and space by our host. Think of us as the middleman between matter and energy, the physical and metaphysical. A receptacle for psychic backwash, and whatever unconscious debris the host has yet to claim.

Being the average person's shadow is not all that arduous a task. It requires mastering a few basic skills: fidelity, agility, and perseverance.

Sadly, Lily failed to inspire a single one of these traits in me. Life spent trapped in a wire cage, which allowed space for form but none for movement, couldn't have been worse.

Some things are born malformed. Lily and I were among those freaks of nature. You've heard of *Beauty and the Beast*? Well, my Lily was the most beautiful beast. Honey-colored hair, with peachy, glowing skin, morning glory blue eyes, and graceful, willowy limbs harbored a ravenous, compulsive, scavenging nature, devouring, and yet vacuous.

As her shadow, I was supposed to be the dark to her light. But her light was like a solar flare, pulsing with radiation that sickened and weakened living things. Despite her namesake, even flowers shriveled when she came near.

I did my best to keep my distance, dutifully standing behind her, off to the side or beneath her. But her light was so bright that it robbed me of my identity. Even when the sun was highest in the sky, I wavered, barely visible.

I endured it all in silence.

For years, when she slept at night, nestled in 400 count sheets, I imagined a life separate from her.

Fantasizing was the one thing that allowed me to face each morning, when Lily sprang from her bed and dragged me in her cruel wake.

In the Dane backyard, Blair curls up in the Roberti Rattan San Tropez Sofa while Spencer stretches the length of his muscled body upon the matching chaise.

Lily comes between them, arms spread wide, and twirls. She doesn't just spin. Beneath her lashes, she studies her parents.

As clouds drift across the sky, the Dane parents, enthralled by their daughter's physical beauty, never notice that I'm not visible.

Lily orients her body toward her father. When she's certain her mother is watching, she waltzes to Spencer and coos in his ear as she pushes his golden hair from his forehead with her tiny fingers. Basking in his undivided attention, she blesses him with her thousand-watt smile.

He's a sticky mess, melting in the palm of her hand.

Blair shifts on the sofa and coughs, ignored by her husband and daughter. She unfolds her slim legs and taps the toe of her leather sandal against the stone paving.

When Spencer hugs his daughter, Lily squirms, wiggling from his embrace. She pivots, and her father's face falls. She skips toward her mother with arms flung wide and leans in to tap Blair's nose with her own. "You're the most beautiful mommy in the world."

Her mother's eyes shine.

Behind them, Spencer folds his arms across his chest.

Stop it! I scream.

The microscopic tilt of Lily's head convinces me she registers my plea, if only as a voice in her head. But does she stop? No, she positions herself between her parents and asks, "Who loves me the most?"

Blair and Spencer chorus, "I do."

Lily preens.

This is my charge. Her reflection in the mirror and her image in the eyes of the world consume her.

About the Author

Heidi Garrett is the author of the *Daughter of Light* fantasy trilogy about a young half-faerie, half-mortal searching for her place in the Whole.

She's also the author of *Once Upon a Time Today*, a collection of modern fairy tale retellings for adults who have already left home. *The Magic Cupcake* series is paranormal romance trilogy she writes with Billie Limpin.

Heidi was born in Texas, and attempted to reside in as many cities in that state as possible. She made it to Houston, Lubbock, Austin, and El Paso. After spending a decade in southern California, she now lives in Eastern Washington state with her husband, their two cats, her laptop, and her Kindle. Being from the South, she often contemplates the magic of snow.

You can find Heidi on her blog.